THE
FACE
OF THE
SHADOW

PART THREE

BOOK OF THE STARS

THE FACE OF THE SHADOW

Erik L'Homme

Translated by Ros Schwartz

SCHOLASTIC INC.

New York   Toronto   London   Auckland   Sydney
Mexico City   New Delhi   Hong Kong   Buenos Aires

ISBN 0-439-65666-4

Original text © 2002 by Gallimard Jeunesse
English translation © 2004 by Ros Schwartz
Illustrations copyright © 2004 by David Wyatt

First published in France in 2002 by Gallimard Jeunesse

Also published in the United Kingdom in 2005 by The Chicken House, 2 Palmer Street, Frome, Somerset BA11 1DS. Email: chickenhouse@doublecluck.com

Cover illustration copyright © 2006 by Mark Zug

Cover design by Elizabeth Parisi

12 11 10 9 8 7 6 5 4 3 2 1   06 07 08 09 10 11

Printed in the U.S.A.

First paperback edition, March 2006

My mother's smile,
My father's gaze.

Coline, Yoann, and Lison, on their island,
Anaïs, Juliette, and Lorraine, on the Web.

CONTENTS

The Story So Far

Thirteen-year-old Robin Penmarch lives on The Lost Isle, a remote land between The Real World and The Uncertain World, where there are computers and cinemas but you're also likely to bump into knights in armor and sorcerers with amazing powers.

When Master Quadehar, the most famous Sorcerer of the Guild, discovers that Robin has a special gift for magic, the boy's destiny is sealed.

While still at school, Robin becomes an apprentice sorcerer, learning the art of magic and the Graphems from his new master. These Graphems, the key to sorcery, were recorded in the *Book of the Stars*. But the precious work was stolen from the Guild many years ago by a young sorcerer called Yorwan, and nobody knows its present whereabouts.

One day, monsters from the terrible Uncertain World suddenly appear on The Lost Isle. Acting on the orders of The Shadow, an evil power, they kidnap Agatha Balangru, the school bully, in front of Robin's eyes. But it is a case of mistaken identity. When Robin, who has been locked up in the forbidding Monastery of Gifdu for his own safety, finds out that The Shadow is actually after him, he decides to escape and go to The Uncertain World to free Agatha. He needs all his rudimentary magic to assist him.

Robin takes his lifelong friends — Amber, Godfrey, Romaric,

and Coral — with him on this risky adventure. But he doesn't get the spell quite right and the five friends are separated. They experience a series of extraordinary adventures and narrow escapes in a world inhabited by many weird and wonderful creatures.

Robin is taken prisoner by the evil Commander Thunku. He meets up with his friends and ultimately with Agatha Balangru in captivity.

Thanks to Master Quadehar's intervention and Robin's magic, the six young people manage to escape and they all return to The Lost Isle safe and sound.

The Guild is alerted and decides to send an expedition to The Uncertain World to find out what is going on. But the sorcerers, led by Quadehar, are ambushed. Meanwhile, the mysterious Lord Sha enters the Monastery of Gifdu, looking for Robin. Lord Sha turns out to be Yorwan, who stole the *Book of the Stars*, in search of his lost son. But he discovers that Robin is not the boy he is seeking.

Master Quadehar is convicted by a court of sorcerers who hold him responsible for the doomed expedition. He is locked up at Gifdu, but with the help of his friend Gerald, he escapes. Convinced that the Guild is harboring a traitor in the pay of The Shadow, he sets off to carry out his own investigation in The Uncertain World and appoints Bertram, a young sorcerer, to keep an eye on Robin.

During a ball in Dashtikazar, the fiery Amber attacks Agatha when she starts flirting with Robin, and chases her onto the moors with her worried friends in hot pursuit. They are all ambushed and captured by the Korrigans, who love playing practical jokes and whose king is determined to hand them over to The Shadow. Eventually, they are freed from the underground kingdom thanks to Robin's cunning and Bertram's cool thinking.

Shortly afterward, Lord Sha summons Robin to The Real World, where he reveals that the *Book of the Stars*, which was supposed to be in his safekeeping, has just been stolen from him. Robin resolves to go and seek Quadehar in The Uncertain World and tell him the whole story, taking only Bertram with him. Lord Sha also confirms that he is not Robin's father, even though he had loved Robin's mother, Alicia.

Robin returns to The Lost Isle more bewildered than ever.

1

ULTIMATUM — THE UNCERTAIN WORLD

The city of Yenibohor, with its forbidding walls towering above The Infested Sea, was the usual hive of activity.

A small group of priests, recognizable by their shaven heads and white robes, surrounded a group of young people walking with bowed heads toward the temple where they were taught to worship Bohor, the evil god of Darkness.

A little further on was a group of Orks wearing the coat of arms of Yadigar, the city of bandits and mercenaries. A priest was handing them a purse containing precious stones in payment for an ambush they had carried out on the orders of the city authorities.

Cries and groans from the many prisoners locked up in the underground cells rose up through the air vents opening on to the street. Most of them were unfortunate souls who had committed the crime of resisting the priests — the rulers of Yenibohor who terrorized the entire Uncertain World.

The men in white robes, the students, and the prisoners had one thing in common: They all shuddered with fear each time they gazed up at the lofty tower that housed the High Priest of the cult of Bohor, The Shadow.

At the top of the imposing keep that was his lair, the unmistakable silhouette of The Shadow paced up and down the flagstone floor of a laboratory crammed with books and instruments. He was furious.

Lomgo, the scribe, still holding the dispatch announcing the bad news, was apprehensive. He huddled against the wall and made himself as inconspicuous as possible, watching fearfully as The Shadow became increasingly agitated. Fragments of darkness detached themselves from his master and sizzled on contact with the stone floor, giving off a choking smell of burning.

Suddenly, The Shadow swung around and glared daggers at the scribe, who cowered even more:

"Escaped! Those cursed Korrigans let him escape! Stupid gnomes . . . incompetent fools . . . traitors . . . my revenge will be terrible!"

The Shadow raised his arms to the heavens and hissed, "So close, so close to my goal. I have the book of spells, all I need is the boy. . . . I can't wait any longer! He must be brought to me. Lomgo . . ."

"Yes, Master!" replied the man, flinging himself to the floor as if imploring the devil's mercy.

"I want my most loyal servants to come out of the darkness. I want the boy . . . at any price. . . . Write to them. I want the boy here in two days, not a day longer. Otherwise I will unleash the full force of my anger against them."

Quaking, the scribe straightened up and shuffled over to his writing desk with hasty little steps.

Behind him, the shape cloaked in shadows had regained an ominous calm. He went over to a table where an immense leather-bound book lay, its cover studded with stars. He turned one of the pages, yellow with age, and pored over a complicated spell.

2

COCKCROW

Robin was fast asleep when his mother opened his bedroom door. The first rays of dawn were beginning to spread their soft light. Alicia gazed at her sleeping son affectionately. He looked so small, so fragile, curled up in bed like that. She found it hard to believe that he had performed the amazing feats he was famed for and she shuddered as she pictured the monsters and bloodthirsty brutes he had been forced to confront in The Uncertain World.

She suddenly felt terribly lonely. The hardest thing was having nobody to lean on, nobody to reassure or comfort her. And worst of all, she always had to be strong. Or at least appear to be. . . .

Alicia took a few steps into the room and sighed. No matter how hard she tried to be the best mother in the world, she could never make up for the man who was missing in their home, the man they both needed so badly. Yorwan . . . whatever had possessed him? Why on earth had he disappeared just a few days before their wedding, without giving any reason? They had been so happy together, so much in love with each other. Yorwan had constantly told her he loved her, and she had seen in his eyes that he meant it. Something must have happened. She was absolutely convinced that something had forced Yorwan to run away and abandon her, unlike Urian, her brother, who had interpreted his sudden disappearance as the action of a coward afraid to commit himself to marriage. And the theft of the Guild's sacred book hadn't exactly helped matters.

She sat down on the edge of the bed and stroked Robin's cheek as he slept. Ultimately, it was he who had suffered most from all these past muddles. She toyed with his chestnut curls for a moment. Then she kissed him. Robin mumbled, but didn't wake up. She gently shook his shoulder.

"Robin, darling . . . it's time to get up."

"Mmm," he groaned, trying to open his eyes. "Is that you, Mom?"

"Who else would it be?" asked Alicia, ruffling his hair.

"Stop it!" he cried, burrowing under the blanket. "Let me sleep a bit longer."

"You can't, Robin. It's daybreak, and your friend Bertram's already waiting for you downstairs."

"Bertram?" Robin exclaimed, poking his tousled head out of the duvet. "Is he here already? But we're not meeting till lunchtime!"

"Well, he must be eager to see you. I wonder what you two are hatching? Come on, hurry up now!"

Alicia rose, opened the window to let in some fresh air and left the room.

Robin groaned. He'd definitely arranged to meet Bertram at

lunchtime when they'd spoken telepathically the day before, near the dolmen. Bertram must have walked all through the night to get there so early. He must be really excited at the prospect of visiting The Uncertain World. Anyway, he was downstairs, and Robin had no time to lose. He leaped up and dived into the bathroom.

A few minutes later, fully dressed and equipped with his precious apprentice sorcerer's bag, he joined Bertram in the kitchen.

"Hi, Bertram! You're up early. It's cockcrow!"

"Hello, Robin," replied the young sorcerer, shaking his hand. "The days are getting shorter and shorter, so I thought we should hurry. . . ."

Bertram, at the grand old age of sixteen, treated everybody condescendingly. It was an act he put on, of course, but sometimes it could be exasperating. His longish honey-colored hair was plastered back. He had dark brown eyes and the straggly beginnings of a goatee and moustache.

"You're going to take a few minutes of your precious time to have a proper breakfast," declared Alicia, in a tone that brooked no argument.

The two friends eagerly tucked into their bread and jam. As soon as they'd drunk their bowls of hot chocolate, they left the table.

"We're going into Dashtikazar for a bit," Robin told his mother. "See you this evening."

"Aren't you coming home for lunch?"

"No, we'll have a sandwich at Father Anselm's."

Alicia didn't insist. She was planning to go riding and could stay out for the afternoon without feeling she had to rush back. She saw the two boys off with an affectionate wave.

"Now tell me everything," urged Bertram, the minute they were alone.

"I've already told you everything," replied Robin. "I absolutely have to tell Master Quadehar something of the utmost importance, and the sooner the better!"

"And what is this 'something'? Can't you tell me?"

"Don't be angry with me, but I want my master to be the first to know."

Bertram didn't press him, but began to whistle. Robin was surprised by his lack of curiosity. Usually, Bertram would have nagged until he let drop a few crumbs of his secret. But that morning, not only was he not insisting, but he didn't even seem put out.

"So how will we get to The Uncertain World?" asked Bertram.

"Using the Desert Galdr. That'll save us having to go all the way to the hill where The Doors are."

"Excellent, excellent," approved Bertram. "But then how will we find Quadehar . . . sorry, Master Quadehar?"

"I'll weave a search spell when we're there," explained Robin. Bertram's trivial questions were beginning to worry him.

"But you know, you can always change your mind," he went on. "You don't have to come with me."

"Change my mind? Don't be silly!" protested Bertram, shocked.

He usually had a smart answer for everything. Robin watched him out of the corner of his eye. Bertram must be exhausted from his night journey from the Monastery of Gifdu not to reply with some clever tease.

They walked over the heath for a while, in the direction of the sea. Then, after looking around to make sure nobody could see them, they invoked the complicated spell that would take them to The Uncertain World. As he recalled the words of the Galdr and the sequence of postures, Robin thought of his friends, Amber, Godfrey, Coral, and Romaric, who until now had taken part in all of his adventures. This was the first time he wasn't taking them with him. Rightly or wrongly, he didn't think he should put them in danger again. He suddenly felt achingly alone, and even Bertram's presence was not enough to comfort him.

When he was ready, he signaled to his companion, who nodded. They held hands. Robin successively adopted the Stadha of the eight Graphems that made up the travel spell, while simultaneously murmuring the corresponding incantation.

Bertram imitated him carefully. It was his first trip to The Uncertain World. There was a sudden flash, followed by the sound of a door opening, and the young sorcerer felt himself being sucked into a powerful whirlwind and hurled into a black void.

The two boys had left The Lost Isle.

≈ ✳ ≈ ✳ ≈

Alicia made her way out of the house in her riding gear. She was about to set out for Urian Penmarch's castle with its stables, where she was meeting a friend, when she saw a figure walking briskly toward her. She recognized the young man at once.

"My humble respects, Mrs. Penmarch. Robin asked me to meet him here at lunchtime. I'm sorry I'm a bit early, but I was so eager to see him again that . . . Is something the matter, Mrs. Penmarch?"

Alicia looked completely baffled.

"But, Bertram, you and Robin left for Dashtikazar not half an hour ago," she said, lamely. "What's all this about?"

"Me? Half an hour ago? You're kidding me!" he replied.

But he could see that she wasn't; she looked utterly mystified.

Suddenly, Alicia's expression changed. She laughed awkwardly, as if at her own stupidity, and wagged her finger at Bertram.

"Oh, very funny. It's one of Robin's stupid pranks. Where is he? Just wait till I get my hands on him!"

"He . . . er, he's . . . ," stammered Bertram.

"All right, that's enough," said Alicia kindly. "What's he forgotten this time? His jacket, I bet."

"Yes, that's it, his jacket."

"It's in his room. Go and get it. I'm going to be late. And tell that lazy son of mine to fetch his own things rather than sending his friends!"

Alicia set off for her brother's castle, wondering what Robin would think of next to wind her up.

Completely baffled, Bertram watched her disappear.

"What does this mean?" puzzled the young sorcerer. "I supposedly arrived earlier, and I left with Robin? Either Robin's mother has gone mad, or something very peculiar is going on."

At first he made as if to walk toward the house, then, as soon as he was out of Alicia's sight, he took to his heels and tore toward Dashtikazar.

3

ROBIN VANISHES

Bertram sank to his knees, exhausted on the muddy path, as the tall white houses of Dashtikazar the Proud, capital of The Lost Isle, came into view. He hadn't caught up with Robin, even though he should easily have done so by now. He had run from the village of Penmarch, which was only a few leagues away. His lungs were burning and his heart was pounding fit to burst. He waited to get his breath back so that he could think clearly.

He left the track and spotted a standing stone that had been split in two by lightning. He sat down beside it.

"Now let's think," Bertram said to himself. "Let's try to analyze the situation rationally: I arrived after Robin had left, and Robin's mother told me she'd seen me with him earlier. That means that someone who looks like me came to Penmarch this morning. He passed himself off as me and took Robin with him. Robin said they were going to Dashtikazar, but they've obviously gone somewhere else. This looks horribly like a kidnapping.

A magic kidnapping even, since both Robin and his mother were taken in by the impostor."

His theory made sense, but he wasn't sure what to do about it. There was not much he could do alone. Who could help him? Master Quadehar had gone off to The Uncertain World with Urian Penmarch and his butler, Valentino, to investigate the massacre of the sorcerers by the Orks at the Tower of Jaghatel.

So who, other than Quadehar, would believe his story of a lookalike and a kidnapping?

The answer was obvious: Robin's friends, who were now Bertram's friends, too, after he had rescued them from the clutches of the Korrigans.

He sat down cross-legged on the ground and wove a Lokk — a magic formula — based on Berkana, the Graphem of communication. First of all, he sent his Lokk to seek out Robin. The lack of a response confirmed his fears: The apprentice was no longer on The Lost Isle. Then he made contact with the first of his friends:

"*Coral? Yoo-hoo! Coral, can you hear me?*"

"What? Who's that? Who's calling me?"

"Is something the matter, Coral?" asked her math teacher sternly. This strict woman did not like any disturbances in her class.

"Don't be cross with her, Miss, she was asleep!" piped up one of the girls in a mocking tone.

"Or she's hearing voices," giggled another.

"Be quiet! Silence!"

The teacher had to bang her metal ruler on the desk several times to restore order.

Coral had a few enemies at Krakal High School. She was

extraordinarily pretty with long, curly chestnut hair and huge blue eyes, and tended to be popular with the boys, which made some of the other girls jealous. She apologized to her teacher and promised it wouldn't happen again. She tried to concentrate on her math exercise, but she was convinced she'd heard a voice. A boy's voice. After all, she wasn't crazy!

"Coral, it's me, Bertram!"

"Bertr . . . ," she began, speaking out loud, before putting her hand in front of her mouth, her eyes round in amazement.

"Shhh! Keep quiet. Just answer me in your head, by concentrating very hard."

"Bertram? But . . . how can it be you?"

"It's magic. Listen carefully, Coral: Robin's been kidnapped. You've got to come and meet me in Dashtikazar. I'm going to contact the others. We'll all meet at The Cockeyed Sailor Inn. Do you know it?"

"Yes, I do. They make great smoothies and . . ."

"Just make sure you tell Amber," Bertram cut her short.

"Don't you want to talk to her yourself?" asked Coral. "Isn't it time you forgave her?"

Coral was referring to the first time Bertram had met the gang . . . the encounter had not gone well for the young sorcerer.

"That's not the reason," he protested, even if he did have painful memories of Amber kneeing him in the stomach. . . . "You know how upset Amber gets when Robin is in danger. . . ."

"Yes, you're right. OK, let me find an excuse to skip class and find my sister. We'll be at the inn at five o'clock, OK?"

"Perfect. See you later."

"Bye, Bertram, and . . ."

Bertram abruptly broke off the telepathic conversation. He was a little bit in love with Coral and now was not the time to get all flustered.

Then he burst into the thoughts of Romaric, who was practicing horsemanship in the paddock at Bromotul Castle, the training school for the Brotherhood of the Knights of the Wind. Romaric was so surprised that he nearly fell off his horse. Even though he wasn't entirely sure how he would get away from Bromotul, Romaric promised Bertram he'd be at The Cockeyed Sailor Inn at five.

After that, Bertram contacted Godfrey during a break in the middle of a rehearsal at the Tantreval Academy of Music where he had been admitted two months earlier. Laid back as usual, Godfrey was not particularly alarmed to hear Bertram's voice inside his head. He, too, assured him he'd be at the rendezvous.

≈ ✳ ≈ ✳ ≈

Exhausted by his long run and the effort of communicating telepathically, Bertram leaned against the standing stone. He drew energy from the ancient menhir. To strengthen its healing power, he summoned Uruz, the Graphem of earth powers, and surrendered himself to its benevolent forces.

When he felt better, he tried to establish a new mental contact. He wove his Lokk and conjured up in his mind the image of his former master, the computer expert at the Monastery of Gifdu.

"Gerald . . . are you there?"

"Where else would I be, Bertram?" replied the sorcerer at once, in a warm, calm voice that soothed the young sorcerer.

16

"I don't know. Maybe off in The Uncertain World, like Master Quadehar. Or you could have disappeared, like Robin . . ."

"What do you mean, disappeared like Robin? Has something happened?"

Bertram explained the situation and told him he suspected that the apprentice sorcerer might have been kidnapped.

"If you are right, that's very serious. You can tell me all about it later. On the other hand, I'm not sure it was such a good idea to have confided in Robin's young friends. They're rather impetuous. But what's done is done . . . I'll pack my bag and leave at once. You say this inn is near the port?"

"Yes. We're all meeting up there at five P.M."

"I'll be there, too. Try and keep everybody calm. A missing apprentice is enough excitement for the time being."

The communication petered out. Bertram let his head loll back against the granite stone. He had done everything he could. Even though Agatha scoffed at his abilities, he knew that when he, Robin, and his friends had found themselves prisoners at the mercy of the Korrigans, it was he, Bertram, who had got them out of a nasty mess.

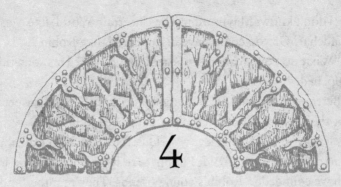

4

THE TRAITOR

Bertram and Robin surfaced in The Uncertain World right in the middle of the Moving Hills. Robin had chosen this place because it was secluded, and because he had been there before.

He took a few steps on the brown grass, blown flat by the blustering wind as if it were froth on the waves. It seemed like only yesterday that he had stood in that same spot all alone, after he and his friends had passed through The Door and been dispersed to all four corners of The Uncertain World.

"We are somewhere between the commercial city of Ferghana in the west, and Yenibohor, the home of the evil priests, in the east. The Infested Sea is to the north, and The Ravenous Desert to the south," he explained to his companion, who knew nothing of this strange and cruel world.

He received no reply. Behind him, Bertram was staggering like a drunkard. Robin wheeled around.

"Bertram, what's wrong? Oh dear, it must be a side effect of the journey between the Worlds. Amber felt like that, too. You'd better lie down until you feel better."

He rushed to support his friend.

But as soon as Robin touched him, Bertram recovered his strength and grabbed him. He held him in an expert stranglehold that made Robin choke.

"Bertram, what . . . you're crazy . . . stop . . ."

Bertram merely snickered and squeezed harder. When he sensed that his victim was on the verge of passing out, he released his grip, just enough to keep him alive. Robin was then amazed to see Bertram's features dissolve into those of an old man. He crumpled to the ground. His head was buzzing. It wasn't true! It was too stupid! He battled against the sinking sensation overcoming him, but in vain. However, he managed instinctively to call up the Graphems using the formula for The Uncertain World and just as he lost consciousness, Gebu and Wunjo began to glow.

≈ ✳ ≈ ✳ ≈

"Quadehar . . . is everything all right?" inquired Urian Penmarch anxiously as the sorcerer came to an abrupt halt.

Urian Penmarch was Robin and Romaric's uncle. A surly giant with a gray beard, he was casually striding along with a fearsome battle-axe over one shoulder and a voluminous bag slung over the other.

"Everything's fine, yes. I just thought for a moment that . . . No, it can't be," muttered Quadehar, shaking his head as if to dispel a sense of foreboding.

Quadehar was Robin's Master Sorcerer. He was built like an athlete, with steel-blue eyes and a tough look that melted when he smiled. He looked about thirty-five or forty. He carried a shoulder bag full of books and magic instruments, and a canvas backpack containing his travel things.

"What's going on?" asked Valentino, Urian's butler and friend. He was a thin, muscular man with white hair who, like his master, wore the turquoise armor of the Knights of the Wind.

"For a second, I thought I'd picked up an SOS. A random spell, like sending a message in a bottle before a shipwreck."

"Were you able to identify the sender?"

"No, Valentino, I didn't have time. It was too brief."

"Could it be . . . a call from Robin?"

"I don't think so, it came from The Uncertain World. . . . Come, let's forget it. Forward march!"

The three men set off again in the direction of the city of the Little Men of Virdu, where they hoped to uncover valuable information about the tragic massacre of Jaghatel.

≈ ✳ ≈ ✳ ≈

The old man bound and gagged Robin, who lay unconscious in the grass of the Moving Hills. He knew what this boy was capable of! Then he shut his eyes and concentrated.

"Master? It's Eusebio, your most willing servant. I have Robin, the boy you want. . . ."

"You have the boy! Congratulations . . . yes, congratulations. . . . You will not be forgotten in my hour of triumph. . . . Where is he? Where is the boy?"

"With me, Master. Somewhere in the Moving Hills."

"Don't say another word. I've located you. . . . I'm sending men . . . to escort you back to me. We'll drink a cider to your success. . . ."

"Thank you, Master. Thank you."

Eusebio of Gri, chief sorcerer of a monastery of the Guild on the Bitter Moor and Quadehar's sworn enemy, waited for the telepathic conversation to end before giving a shudder. Even at a distance, the voice of the demon cloaked in shadows made his blood run cold. He tested the reliability of his captive's bonds one last time, then settled down to wait impatiently for the arrival of his master's men.

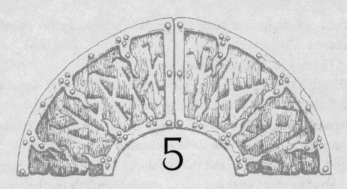

5

THE COCKEYED SAILOR INN

Bertram arrived at the port of Dashtikazar early. To pass the time, he wandered among the sturdy fishing boats and the yachts belonging to the city's wealthy families.

The shrill cries of the gulls battling against the breeze mingled with the flapping of loose sails and the jingling of the shrouds against the masts.

Bertram felt a pang of sadness. This harbor reminded him of another port, somewhere in The Real World, where he used to go on holiday with his parents as a child. He remembered the beach, and playing ball with his father while his mother sunbathed on a white towel. . . . All that was so far away, it felt like a previous life, before the accident in which his parents had died, before his godfather, Gerald, had brought him back to The Lost Isle.

He felt a lump in his throat, and his eyelids fluttered. He reprimanded himself for being so sentimental, took a handkerchief out of his pocket, and blew his nose. Then he strode toward the inn where he was to meet the others.

All sorts of people gathered at The Cockeyed Sailor Inn. In the mornings, fishermen and fish merchants haggled over a glass of fruity wine from the Golden Mountains. At lunchtime, the local traders gathered over a cider, a platter of shellfish, or a poached wing of skate with capers, to talk shop. In the afternoons, students liked to sit in the alcoves of the spacious restaurant to work or chat, drinking endless smoothies and coffees. The evenings brought together a mixed crowd of regulars who would philosophize about the world, then launch into ribald drinking songs.

When Bertram pushed open the door, he was greeted by the stares of a handful of students. They did not often have the chance to see a member of the Guild dressed in the prestigious dark cloak of the sorcerer and carrying the mysterious bag.

His arrival clearly astonished two people in particular, who hastily concealed themselves in an alcove from which muffled exclamations could soon be heard.

Bertram, apparently unaware of these odd goings-on, sat down at a round table near the door.

The hands on the clock above the counter were on the dot of five when two girls made their entrance. They looked about thirteen, and were alike as two peas in a pod, except that one wore her hair short and the other long.

"Amber! Coral!" called Bertram, waving at them.

"Hello, Bertram! It's great to see you," exclaimed the lovely Coral, planting two smacking kisses on the cheeks of the blushing sorcerer.

"Hi," said Amber, coolly holding out her hand. "You look as though you've caught the sun!"

Amber was Coral's twin sister. While Coral was feminine and

coquettish, Amber was sporty and strong-willed. Boys adored Coral and were in awe of her sister. But there were chinks in Amber's armor; sometimes, when her defenses were down, her feelings for Robin made her very vulnerable.

"That's good, you're on time," Bertram welcomed them. "I've contacted Romaric and Godfrey; they weren't sure if they could get here at five, but they promised to come."

"Right, now tell us what's going on," demanded Amber, sitting down.

"Let's order first," suggested Coral, trying to catch the waiter's attention. "What are you having? Amber? Bertram?"

"A hot chocolate."

"An apple cider."

"And a strawberry smoothie for me," added Coral.

"Another apple cider, please."

Bertram, Amber, and Coral turned to look at the breathless, perspiring man who had spoken to the waiter.

"Gerald!" exclaimed Bertram, visibly delighted.

Short, bald, and bespectacled, Gerald had the paunch of a man who clearly enjoyed his food. There was an intelligent gleam in his sharp eyes. A great friend of Quadehar's, he was about forty and wore the dark cloak and carried the bag of the Sorcerers of the Guild.

Bertram hastily made the introductions:

"Gerald, meet Amber and Coral, friends of Robin's. They come from Krakal. Girls, this is Gerald, my Master Sorcerer and godfather. Given the gravity of the situation, I took the liberty of inviting him to join us."

Amber and Coral had politely risen to their feet.

"We're very pleased to meet you."

"And I'm pleased to meet you, young ladies," replied Gerald, mopping his brow. "Please, let's sit down. I'm exhausted from my journey, and I think I've already created enough of a stir!"

The conversations around them that had stopped for a moment resumed all the louder. Two sorcerers in The Cockeyed Sailor Inn in one day — now that created a buzz of excitement!

The waiter brought the drinks. They clinked glasses.

After taking a few sips of the excellent cider made from delicious Lost Isle apples and honey, Gerald gave a contented sigh.

"That's better!" he exclaimed. "The journey from Gifdu has worn me out. . . . By the way, Bertram, I thought you said all of your friends were coming."

"Yes, but Romaric has to find a way of escaping from the fortress school of Bromotul, and Godfrey from the Tantreval Academy. It's not as simple as that."

They decided to wait for the others before discussing the important issues, despite Amber's growing impatience. They chatted about this and that and, at last, just when they were beginning to despair of Romaric and Godfrey turning up, the two boys burst into the inn.

Romaric was Robin's cousin, and his senior by a few months. He was thirteen and a half, but looked older. A sturdy, muscular boy, he was brave and determined. His fair hair and intense blue eyes were the hallmarks of a true Penmarch.

Godfrey was the same age as Romaric, give or take a few days, and was his best friend. Tall and lanky, he had hazel eyes and black hair, which was always immaculately groomed. He had an abrasive humor and an imperturbable calm, and was studying to be a musician.

The two boys apologized to their friends; it had been really difficult to get away from their teachers and custodians. They were delighted to meet Gerald, the famous godfather who had brought Bertram back to The Lost Isle. They ordered two glasses of iced cranberry juice and sat down.

"Excellent. Now that we're all here . . ." began Bertram.

"At last!" groaned Amber, who was, by now, beside herself with anxiety about Robin's disappearance.

"Be quiet, Amber," chided Romaric.

He and the others had not forgotten the scene she had made on the heath, when the Korrigans had attacked Robin.

"For goodness' sake, don't start arguing," said Bertram with irritation. "Let me remind you that Robin has disappeared and that he's probably been kidnapped, so let's focus our energy on finding him."

Calm was restored. They all listened attentively as Bertram described what had happened and explained the conclusions he had drawn. The listeners were shocked. They were so absorbed in Bertram's story that they were unaware that their conversation seemed to be of great interest to two people in a neighboring alcove, the same pair who had stared round-eyed when Bertram had walked in. . . .

"I can confirm one thing," declared Gerald, "and that is that Robin is no longer on The Lost Isle. I tried to contact him telepathically, but I wasn't able to."

"The Shadow!" exclaimed Coral. "It has to be him!"

"It's possible. In fact it's even highly likely," admitted Gerald.

He couldn't help thinking about the traitor hiding — at least so Quadehar and he himself believed — within the Guild itself.

"In any case, it is someone who is sufficiently acquainted with the sorcerer's art to be able to alter his appearance," he added.

"Is that possible?" asked Romaric in amazement.

"Of course!" replied Bertram in a superior tone. "You just have to . . ."

"Oh, for goodness' sake, the question is not how, nor even who, but where? Where has Robin been taken?" broke in Godfrey.

"To The Uncertain World, most likely, seeing as Bertram didn't catch up with them on the road to Dashtikazar, or on the hill where The Doors are," replied Gerald. "Now the Desert Galdr, as you know from having used it with Master Quadehar, only allows you to go from The Lost Isle to The Uncertain World."

"So what are we waiting for?" asked Romaric. "Let's go there."

"Whoa! Whoa!" said Gerald in an authoritative tone, raising his hands in disapproval. "You're not going anywhere! The situation is complicated enough as it is. Don't make it worse. You are all going to return home quietly. Meanwhile, I shall go straight to see the Provost. He will decide on the best course of action."

Gerald rose. Amber was about to argue with the sorcerer when Romaric signaled to her to keep quiet.

Gerald paid the bill and said good-bye to the friends.

"Bertram," he said at length, "I'm relying on you to make sure that these young people don't do anything foolish. All right? Excellent. Good-bye!"

"Good-bye!" they chorused.

As soon as the sorcerer had left, they exchanged glances.

"Do you know what I think?" asked Romaric, pretending to examine his fingernails.

His friends grinned knowingly, and Bertram looked disapproving.

6

A RECKLESS DECISION

"What do you think?" asked Romaric after laying out his plan.

"Suits me," said Amber, nodding. "Suits me fine."

"Robin is in danger. We can't sit here twiddling our thumbs!" agreed Godfrey.

"Oh . . . as long as I'm with all of you," was all Coral said, sneaking a glance at Romaric.

They all turned to look at Bertram, who didn't breathe a word.

"What about you, Bertram?" asked Romaric.

"Sorry, but there's one flaw in your plan," replied the young man.

"Oh really? What?" Romaric demanded.

"To get to The Uncertain World, you have to open The Door to The Uncertain World. So you need a sorcerer . . ."

"And you're not a sorcerer?" retorted Amber.

"Yes, I'm a sorcerer," he replied. "But who said I'd agree to help you? My godfather asked me to make sure you didn't do anything stupid. And your plan to go and find Robin in The Uncertain World sounds stupid to me!"

"Deserter," accused Godfrey.

"Deserter? Traitor, more like!" fumed Amber, glowering at Bertram.

"Shut up!" interrupted Romaric. "Bertram's right. Without his help we're stuck here."

"What do we have to do to make you change your mind? Get down on our knees and beg?" asked Amber nastily.

"I confess I'd rather enjoy that," Bertram replied with a half-smile. "But it's no use. Romaric's plan is too dangerous, and that's all there is to it."

"And if I kissed you?" offered Coral. "Girls always kiss the heroes to spur them on."

"I'd rather enjoy that, too!" said Bertram with a mischievous gleam in his eye. "But . . ."

"Oh! Forget it," sighed Romaric, giving Godfrey a discreet kick under the table. "In any case, it's a totally ridiculous plan. . . ."

"Ridiculous? What do you mean, ridiculous?" flared Amber. "I think it's brilliant . . ."

"I said ridiculous," repeated Romaric, stopping her short, "because it's clear that even if he wanted to, Bertram would be utterly incapable of opening The Door to The Uncertain World."

Taken aback, Bertram gasped.

"But it's not his fault," added Godfrey, giving Romaric a knowing look. "Not everyone has the skill to open The Doors on the hill."

"But . . . but I . . ."

"It's true," went on Romaric. "I've heard that only the very best sorcerers have the magic power to pull off that amazing feat."

"Bertram is an ace sorcerer!" protested Coral in his defense.

"Quite right!" exclaimed Bertram, deeply offended. "I'm perfectly capable of opening The Door to The Uncertain World. I'll prove it to you this very afternoon."

"Yesss!" whooped Godfrey before Bertram could change his mind. "That's the Bertram we know. Let's drink to our hero!"

"To Bertram! And to Robin, who we are going to rescue!" They clinked glasses and mugs. Bertram puffed out his chest like a peacock.

"Right, let's not waste time," said Amber. "Let's go. Robin might be in serious danger."

"That's true," agreed Romaric, jumping up. "Come on!"

Just then, they heard a voice behind them.

"Sorry you guys, but . . ."

". . . you're not going anywhere without us!"

They swung around. Bursting out of the alcove where they'd been hiding, Agatha Balangru and Thomas Kandarisar stood before them with determined expressions on their faces.

Agatha was a tall, rather skinny girl with dark eyes and hair, and a mouth that was too big for her face. Like her sidekick, Thomas, she was coming up on her fourteenth birthday. She had once been Robin's sworn enemy at school, before she had been kidnapped by Gommons. But then Robin and his friends had rescued her, and she'd developed a crush on the apprentice sorcerer, which infuriated Amber.

Thomas, a stocky, sturdy boy with red hair who tended to sulk, was Agatha's best friend. Robin had saved him from the clutches of a monster, and since that episode his gratitude had known no bounds.

"Thomas? Agatha? What are you two doing here?" asked Romaric in surprise.

"We had a history test this afternoon," replied Agatha. "Thomas and I weren't quite ready for it, so we decided to skip it. What a stroke of luck bumping into you!"

"And Agatha recognized Bertram when he came in," added Thomas.

"We gathered something was going on, so we decided to stick around," she went on.

"And a good thing we did, too," said Thomas. "We heard everything!"

"So there you are," said Agatha, crossing her arms defiantly. "Either you let us in on the action or we'll tell the Provost's guards all we know."

There was silence. They stared at each other, wondering what to do next. Then, seeing that Agatha and Thomas meant business, Romaric sat down again and invited the others to do likewise.

"I warn you, we'll be taking risks," said Romaric. "It'll be dangerous."

"Robin has never hesitated to come to our aid, even when it was dangerous," replied Agatha. "Has he, Thomas?"

"It's true," agreed the redhead. "He could have saved his own skin that day when we were chased by the Gommon on the beach, but he turned back to come and help us. . . . He didn't have to do that."

"OK, fine," stated Romaric. "We're all indebted to Robin."

Amber scowled.

"I don't trust Agatha's motives," she declared.

"Listen, Amber," replied Agatha, turning pink. "I admit I behaved badly during the Samain holidays in Dashtikazar. But I've sworn, and everybody here is a witness, that I . . . that I'm not interested in Robin anymore."

"It's true, she did swear, Amber," echoed Coral.

"Let's be honest," chipped in Godfrey. "Seven will hardly be too many to save Robin from the clutches of his kidnapper."

"Godfrey's right," said Thomas. "Let's stop quarreling. What matters right now is Robin's life."

"Besides, I don't think we're exactly prepared for a trip to The Uncertain World," said Agatha. "We'd do well to drop into my place first to pick up some supplies."

Bertram said nothing. He had turned very pale.

"Bertram? Are you OK?" asked Coral.

"Yes . . . ," he mumbled. "It's just that . . . er . . . opening The Door isn't easy and . . . and I don't know if I'm capable of taking six people. . . ."

"We trust you absolutely, Bertram the Sorcerer," said Amber, clapping his shoulder affectionately.

"You're the best!" added Coral, fluttering her eyelashes.

"Under your protection, I'm sure we can fight The Shadow himself," added Agatha.

"OK then, come on!" exclaimed Bertram, leaping to his feet, suddenly bucking up. "What are we waiting for? Let's go!"

7

THE COSMIC SPHERE

R obin came to his senses on the cold flagstone floor of a dark
room. It took a moment for him to collect his wits. He felt
as though he was coming back from a far-off place, and even
trying to think hurt his head. What had happened? Bertram had
come to meet him at his house in Penmarch, and they had set off
over the heath. But was it really Bertram? If not, then who was
it? And where had they been going? Oh yes, they had been on
their way to The Uncertain World, in search of Master Quadehar.
But something had happened. . . . Suddenly, everything came
flooding back: Bertram strangling him, Bertram turning into a
snickering old man.

With a huge effort, Robin managed to ease himself into a sitting position. As his eyes got used to the dark, he could see a
vast, circular room that was bare except for a straw mattress,
a blanket, and a pitcher of water. A barred skylight let in a little
daylight and gave an idea of the thickness of the walls, built, like
the floor, from enormous blocks of gray stone. Finally, a heavy

wooden door with iron fittings was the only way out of the cell. For it was indeed a prison cell.

A voice broke into the silence.

"The floor of your cell wasn't too hard to sleep on, I hope?"

Robin jumped and looked in the direction of the door. It was ajar. It took him a few moments to make out the figure of a man framed in the doorway. He recognized the old man who had passed himself off as Bertram.

The Chief Sorcerer of Gri spat on the ground and chortled.

"I'd hate to think you were uncomfortable, Robin the Great, Hero of the Sorcerers of the Guild, the favorite pupil of that fool Quadehar!"

Robin struggled to his feet. His head wasn't hurting quite so badly, and the feeling of giddiness had passed.

"Who are you?"

"I am first and foremost the humble servant of the Master of this World. And of The Lost Isle," he added sarcastically. "I play the part of Chief Sorcerer in the Monastery of Gri . . ."

"You are a sorcerer!" exclaimed Robin. "You used magic to impersonate Bertram, but how —"

The Chief Sorcerer of Gri interrupted him with a mocking gesture.

"Little fool . . . you didn't think you knew everything about sorcery after six months' apprenticeship, did you? Raidhu is not only the chariot, it is also the means of transformation. Dagaz makes it possible to hide one's identity, Fehu to create a new image for oneself, and Uruz to stabilize it. The rest is merely a matter of weaving a spell. . . ."

"I already know all that," replied Robin, shrugging his

shoulders. "I was simply wondering how you knew that Bertram was coming to see me."

Visibly taken aback, the Chief Sorcerer paused. The apprentice's words and the calm way he had spoken had shaken him. What audacity, what self-assurance this young boy had! Was the Master right? Was Robin Penmarch capable of unlocking the ultimate spells of the Great Book?

"I intercepted your mental conversation the other night," explained the sorcerer tersely. "I wasn't planning to eavesdrop, but you projected your Lokk toward Bertram with such force that I couldn't help but hear. Now, that's enough," he said abruptly, making as if to leave. "The Master will be coming to see you shortly. And I must return to The Lost Isle and turn back into the Chief Sorcerer of Gri. We don't want the Guild to become suspicious!"

He laughed mirthlessly.

The door closed behind the elderly sorcerer and Robin found himself alone again. He suddenly felt profoundly despondent. It had cost him a great effort to put on a brave face in front of the Chief Sorcerer of Gri. Now he was alone, Robin could let go. Despair swept over him. This time, he was done for. He was well and truly the prisoner of none other than The Shadow himself. Nobody knew where Robin was, so nobody would ever come and rescue him. He was lost. Then the words of Kor Mehtar, the Korrigan king, came back to him, and he felt very afraid: "You'll suffer a fate that's worse than death," he'd said on the moor, when he decided he'd hand Robin over to The Shadow.... What did this evil character want of him? And above all, what was he going to do to him? Fighting his tears,

Robin went over to the mattress and slumped onto it. Then he closed his eyes and wished with all his might that this were just a bad dream.

≋ ✳ ≋ ✳ ≋

When he opened his eyes again, a long time had gone by. He had fallen into a very deep sleep from which he emerged groggily. A glance around confirmed that, sadly, this was no bad dream.

He dragged himself to his feet. He hadn't escaped the Gommons, or confronted the Orks, or beaten off Thunku to end up in this wretched cell, in the clutches of The Shadow. He had to do something. Anything, as long as he fought back. Even if it was hopeless.

He thought of his master, and that inspired him. On reflection, he realized that he wasn't completely helpless. Since he'd been practicing magic, he had pulled off some amazing stunts. Bertram had told him so, and so had Gerald. Robin had even managed to stand up to Lord Sha with the help of a Lokk he had concocted. He was going to show The Shadow what he could do! But . . . where to begin?

Robin decided to proceed methodically, without wasting a moment. He wove a communication Lokk and projected it toward Quadehar, whose face he had conjured up in his mind. The Lokk boomeranged straight back and hit his mind with a little thud.

Surprised, Robin repeated it several times before it dawned on him: A spell had been cast on the walls of his cell to prevent communication. Which meant that even if his master knew that he was in The Uncertain World and was trying to find him, he wouldn't be able to make contact with him.

"OK, at least I know now," Robin said to himself. "I know I'll have to do this on my own."

After some thought, he decided to weave a defensive spell, putting himself under the protection of the Armor of Elhaz combined with a Helmet of Terror. He knew that this would not be enough; The Shadow had awesome powers. But it was better than nothing. So he moved to the center of the cell, taking with him the blanket and the pitcher.

"If my protection works, I'll need water to survive the siege," he said out loud, comforted by the sound of his own voice. Then he thought about how to draw the Graphems for the spell on the ground; his captor had taken away his apprentice's bag containing his Ristir — the sorcerer's knife normally used for this purpose. Luckily, the old Chief Sorcerer of Gri hadn't had the presence of mind to remove Robin's belt. He undid it, and with the metal buckle, he engraved the Helmet of Terror Lokk six times around him and the objects he had assembled. When he had finished, he uttered the incantation that would create a protective wall of invisible energy around him:

"By the power of Elhaz, Erda, and Kari, Rind, Hir, and Loge, Egishjamur in front, Egishjamur behind, Egishjamur to the left, Egishjamur to the right, Egishjamur above, and Egishjamur below, Egishjamur protect me! ALU!"

To his great satisfaction, the air quivered around him.

"Perfect! It seems to be working! So The Shadow isn't using any blocking magic like in the Korrigans' cave."

He began to feel a little better. He was no longer totally vulnerable. But he was going to have to find an even more powerful protection than the Armor and the Helmet to stand up to The Shadow.

"Right. My Galdr is only a first line of defense. I've built the walls of my castle, now I need a keep. That's what I need, a keep! What could I use?"

He racked his brains in vain. He was about to give up and make do with just the protection he had, when three of the twenty-four Graphems he had called, which were lined up in his mind, timidly began to glow. In the same way as Thursaz had appeared when he had confronted the Gommon on the beach on The Lost Isle, and Isaz had acted almost of its own accord under the wagon of the phony magician Gordogh in Ferghana, the Graphems Odala, Hagal, and Mannaz presented themselves automatically.

"Odala, the Graphem of possession, protector of the home . . . Of course! Why didn't I think of that to reinforce my Armor?"

He hastily drew the form of Odala between each Egishjamur, making sure to adapt it to the form used in The Uncertain World. Then he murmured a spell to control it:

"*You, the heritage, the gift of evening, you who govern sacred places, because in your domain the eagle is safe, help me to strengthen my walls! OALU!*"

When the sixth drawing was complete and the circle closed, the image of Odala glowed darkly and projected a translucent blue light onto the wall of energy which had been invisible until then. It seemed to Robin that the walls had tripled in thickness. He was delighted.

"Right, now that I have a wall that can be called a wall, let's build the keep!"

The apprentice called the second Graphem, which had shyly come forward, and which was perhaps the most powerful of all: Hagal. Master Quadehar had once told him that all of the mysteries of the multiverse were perhaps locked up in its eight branches. The sorcerers affectionately called it the Great Mother, or the Star. In this case, Hagal would make the perfect keep.

He drew a single, giant Hagal covering the entire surface inside the Armor. Then he sat down in the center of the Graphem and invoked its protection:

"You, the hail, you the red, daughter of Ymir, because Hropt loved the Ancient World, I put myself in your hands! HALU!"

The ground beneath Robin trembled slightly. Then the eight branches of the Graphem began to crackle and blaze, sending up cold red tongues of flame.

"Perfect!" cried Robin. "Now let The Shadow come!"

He dismissed the Graphems from his mind. They all faded, except Mannaz, the last one, which had glowed faintly a few moments earlier. This odd behavior baffled Robin. It was definitely trying to tell him something. He had built a wall and a keep — what else could he do?

The answer suddenly dawned on him: He needed a refuge, a secret room at the heart of the keep. A last resort, an ultimate hiding place. He knelt down and, in the center of Hagal, he drew Mannaz, the twentieth Graphem, the cosmic sphere, the link between humans and the powers. Then he whispered to activate the Graphem, as you had to when several magic signs were being asked to work together, or side by side:

"You, the link, brother of Mani, stellar sphere, ancestor of the hundred doctors, dreams, and the unconscious, unity of time,

*because powerful is the falcon's talon, I place my trust in you!
MALU!"*

Nothing spectacular happened, but Mannaz then sank several inches into the stone onto which it had been engraved.

Robin had done everything possible. Suddenly feeling desperately thirsty, he gulped a few mouthfuls of water from the pitcher, then forced himself to put it down again. Now that he had effectively declared war on The Shadow, he had to use his few resources sparingly.

8

A SEA OF TURQUOISE ARMOR

The Provost's palace rose up on the summit of one of the seven hills that gave the town of Dashtikazar, nestling in the bay, a unique aspect. Gerald crossed the main square, where ceremonies and festivals took place, and climbed the monumental steps to the building where the supreme authority on The Lost Isle lived and worked.

Gerald was genuinely concerned. He waved absentmindedly to the knight standing sentry in front of the main door, who saluted him respectfully, then set off down the corridors leading to the office of the man who was both mayor of Dashtikazar and prefect of the entire country.

The Provost was a tallish, middle-aged man with gimlet eyes and white hair, which he wore brushed back. When he was younger, he had been a Qamdar, a wise and respected clan chief, and he had been voted Provost by an overwhelming majority of the population. The Provost was among the most powerful figures on The Lost Isle, alongside the Commander of the Brotherhood, the

Craftsmen and Tradesmen's representative, and the Chief Sorcerer of the Guild. He was also the most legitimate because, unlike the others, he had been elected by the people. But he was also the most vulnerable, for the people of The Lost Isle could just as easily take power away from him and replace him should a new majority wish to, and have good reason for doing so.

Informed of Gerald's arrival by an assistant, the Provost came and opened the door himself. The computer specialist rarely left Gifdu and, when he did so, it was always for an important reason.

"Come in, Gerald. To what do we owe this honor? Do sit down."

Gerald sank into the leather armchair indicated by the Provost, while his host returned to his chair at his desk.

"Very well. What's the matter?"

"Your Honor, I'm afraid that our worst fears have been realized. Robin was kidnapped this morning and is at this very moment in The Uncertain World."

A furrow of profound annoyance creased the Provost's brow.

"How could that have happened? Wasn't Quadehar with him?"

"There are a number of things I have to explain, Your Honor . . . ," began Gerald awkwardly.

And he told the astonished Provost about the Guild's plan to attack The Shadow in his lair, the resulting massacre at the Tower of Jaghatel, the trial that had found Quadehar guilty, the Master Sorcerer's escape to Penmarch, and his departure for The Uncertain World with Urian and Valentino.

The Provost was furious.

"This is unbelievable! How can such important events take place without my being informed? Do you have any idea how serious this is?"

"I'm fully aware of it, Your Honor," said Gerald quietly, trying to appease the Provost. "I know perfectly well that the Guild has gone too far. But there's no changing that now. We must act, and quickly!"

"Very well, but what is it you fear? What's likely to happen if Robin falls into the hands of The Shadow?"

"To be honest, I don't know," confessed the sorcerer.

"What do you mean, you don't know?" asked the Provost in dismay.

"It's the truth, Your Honor," Gerald went on, looking him straight in the eye. "But there's one thing I'm certain of, and that is that the boy has outstanding magic powers. There's no doubt that if The Shadow is so desperate to get his hands on Robin, it's to use his powers for evil purposes. It is therefore essential to find him before that happens."

The Provost thought for a moment, then he rose and strode over to the door.

"It's too great a responsibility for me," he announced. "I'm going to call a meeting of the Supreme Council at once."

"Don't do that, I beg you!" cried Gerald.

The Provost turned and shot Gerald a look of utter bafflement.

"It is essential for this business to remain a secret between us," the sorcerer went on, biting his lip. "Please trust me."

"You're not making any sense, Gerald," snapped the Provost.

"Quadehar and I believe that there is at least one traitor in the Guild. . . ."

The Provost continued to stare at him, flabbergasted.

"This gets better and better!" he spluttered finally. "So what do you suggest?"

Gerald thought for a moment. "Your Honor, I can see only one solution. Do you trust the Commander of the Brotherhood?"

"Well, he's a straightforward, trustworthy fellow, unschooled in the subtle ways of politics, but he's upright and totally devoted to his mission as a knight. Yes, I trust him."

"The Guild and the Brotherhood have always had respect for each other, but they rarely see eye to eye, and there is little love lost between them," said Gerald. "In my view, that is a useful guarantee. I believe that the Brotherhood, unlike the Guild, has not been tainted by The Shadow's scheming."

"Perfect," concluded the Provost, opening the door and beckoning the sentry in the corridor. "I shall send for the Commander at once, and request that he use the utmost discretion."

"Tell him to act fast!" begged Gerald. "I repeat, this is an emergency. The Lost Isle's future may depend on it!"

"Sadly, I fear that it might not be possible to do anything until tomorrow morning," replied the Provost, turning toward him. "It is already late, and organizing a large-scale operation takes time."

The sorcerer sighed. Time was against them.

≈ ✳ ≈ ✳ ≈

It was the coldest hour of the night, just before daybreak. Hugging his cloak around him, Gerald jumped up and down on the spot to keep warm.

In the event, the Provost had acted swiftly: Nearly two hundred knights were assembled with their weapons and belongings on the hill where The Doors stood, and a sea of turquoise armor glinted in the pale dawn light. The Provost and the Commander came over to the sorcerer.

"These are the men who will accompany us to The Uncertain World," announced the Commander of the Knights of the Brotherhood in a gruff voice. "It's all I can do. It would be a mistake to empty The Lost Isle of all its knights. The Shadow might take advantage. . . ."

The Commander was a giant of a man, similar in stature to Urian Penmarch. Like Gerald, he was over forty. His craggy face bore countless scars. He was a valiant knight who had proved his mettle many times on the battlefields.

The Provost nodded his agreement and then continued.

"The Commander will be in charge of the operation. But you, Gerald, will be the guide, and he will not undertake anything without consulting you."

"That suits me," replied Gerald, looking directly at the Commander. "I know I can trust you, Commander. You have proved your loyalty on numerous occasions when The Shadow has attacked The Lost Isle. Your men respect you, and so shall I."

Touched by Gerald's friendly words, the knight proffered his hand. The sorcerer shook it and thanked him for taking charge of the operation personally.

"It is my duty and my privilege to be in the front line with my men," replied the Commander modestly.

"Right," broke in the Provost, to halt this exchange of courtesies. "Gerald, what are we waiting for?"

"Getting two hundred knights through The Door is no easy matter," Gerald explained with an amused smile. "I have asked the only available sorcerer in whom I can place my absolute trust to come and help me. He should be here any minute."

A few moments later, they could see a figure silhouetted on top of the hill. Soon they were able to identify an elderly man wearing the dark cloak of the Guild perched on the back of a reluctant mule. He drew nearer, coaxing and scolding his wheezing mount.

"That's the last time I make the journey from Gifdu on the back of such a stubborn animal!" he complained on arrival.

"Qadwan! What a pleasure to see you!" exclaimed Gerald, clapping him on the back.

Qadwan was the gym master at Gifdu. Although he was elderly, he was extremely spry for his age.

"So, you decided to come?" Gerald asked him.

"Do you think I hesitated for a second? Knowing Robin is in danger makes my blood boil! Besides, when a friend needs help . . ."

"And I do, believe me. Getting this Door open will be no picnic!"

Followed by the Provost and the Commander, the two sorcerers walked toward The Door to The Uncertain World. The massed knights gazed after them with a mixture of curiosity and apprehension.

Gerald and Qadwan stood on either side of the monumental Door. Then Gerald addressed the knights:

"We are going to open The Door fully, not just a little way, as we usually do. We mustn't lose any time. You will file through one by one, without hesitation, and on the double. Like parachutists in The Real World jumping out of a plane."

The men laughed and relaxed a little.

"Right, who wants to go first?" asked Qadwan.

"Me," said a slim, fair-haired knight, stepping forward.

"Me, too!" echoed a stocky, dark-haired fellow, falling in behind the first.

"Ambor and Bertolen!" exclaimed the commander, with a little smile. "I'm not surprised."

"Shall we go?" asked Gerald, with an inquiring glance at the Provost.

"Yes, it is time," he replied, with heartfelt emotion in his voice. "May the Graphems watch over you, Master Sorcerers! May the wind of the moors go with you, Commander! And above all, good luck!"

"We'll need it," sighed Gerald, invoking the Graphems.

9

THOMAS TAKES CHARGE OF
THE SITUATION

"I'm hungry!" whined Coral.

"You should have eaten a real lunch," retorted Romaric.

"I wasn't hungry then. Oh, Romaric, don't be mean! Just give me a sandwich."

"But Coral, we said we'd wait until we reached The Uncertain World before eating anything. Come on, be patient."

"Will you two get a move on?" chided Amber irritably, turning to her sister and Romaric, who were lagging behind the others.

"OK, we're coming," grumbled Coral. "It's not my fault if my backpack weighs a ton! And besides, why don't you moan at Bertram? He's even further behind!"

Bertram was indeed dawdling, and his face wore a hangdog expression. He did not seem in a great hurry to catch up with them.

"Can you speed up a little, Bertram? Thank you!" exclaimed Amber.

"Yes, yes, I'm coming," replied the sorcerer touchily, without moving any faster.

≋ ✳ ≋ ✳ ≋

The little group had left Dashtikazar in the afternoon. The day before, Agatha had taken them to her parents' luxurious house in a residential district of the capital. She had ransacked her father's wardrobe for warm clothing for the boys and allowed the twins to take their pick from her own. Then she had raided the fridge and the pantry, and rummaged through the shed where the camping equipment was kept.

By the time they were equipped, it was already dark. So they slept on the thick carpet of Agatha's vast bedroom, snug in the sleeping bags and blankets they'd taken from the shed.

Apart from Bertram, who remained aloof, the group had talked at length about their adventures with Robin on The Lost Isle and in The Uncertain World.

Needless to say, they woke up late and eventually, after a hearty breakfast which only Coral had declined, they had set off for the hill where The Doors stood.

≋ ✳ ≋ ✳ ≋

"We'll soon be within sight of The Doors," announced Godfrey, dropping his voice slightly. "We'd better make less noise."

"Did you hear that?" Amber asked her sister, darting a furious look at her.

Coral mimed sewing up her lips to show that from now on she would keep her mouth shut.

They plodded on in silence until they reached the big rock behind which some of them had hidden last summer, while they were waiting for Robin to cast his spell over the guards. Then they scanned the surrounding area: A lone knight was guarding the two Doors.

"A piece of cake!" crowed Amber. "Bertram will call up the Graphem that makes time stand still and it'll be easy. We'll walk past the sentry as if we were invisible, won't we, Bertram?"

"Hmm . . ."

"What do you mean, hmm?"

The young sorcerer swallowed uneasily.

"Well, I . . . I've never used that Graphem before and I don't know whether . . ."

"Remind me, Amber, it *is* Bertram who's supposed to open The Door to The Uncertain World, isn't it?" said Romaric.

"Yes, and I promise you he'll do it!" Amber replied.

"Back off," pleaded Bertram. "The Door is . . . actually, it's easier."

"Are you kidding us?" asked Agatha.

"No," he sighed. "I can't explain it, but using a Graphem in midair is much more complicated than activating a Graphem carved on a Door."

"I have the feeling that you're not telling us everything . . . ," said Godfrey in a suspicious tone.

"Yes, I am, well . . . no-no, all right!" stammered the sorcerer. "I know I can summon the Graphems on the Door . . . but after that, I don't know whether my Ond — you know, my inner energy — will be powerful enough to open it."

"And when will you know that?" retorted Amber, trying to control her temper.

"Once I touch The Door . . ."

"And the thing with the knight, you know, the thing to freeze him like a statue?" asked Coral. "Can you really not do it? I thought that was amazing!"

"I think . . . think it's best to forget the whole thing," muttered Bertram, hanging his head.

"No way!" protested Romaric. "We're not going to give up before we've even started!"

"So what exactly have you in mind?" Agatha snapped, cuttingly. "Our only hope was this sorcerer who's clearly only of any use when he can wave a gun around. And now he doesn't even have a gun anymore, he tossed it into the sea!"

"Don't be so harsh!" cried Coral. "Don't forget he did save our lives when we were captured by the Korrigans. . . ."

"Shut up and let Romaric handle it," hissed her sister.

Romaric threw his hands up in a gesture of helplessness. He couldn't think of any alternative.

Then Thomas spoke:

"We'll have to jump him and tie him up like a sausage."

"Excuse me?" replied Godfrey, shocked.

"No way!" said Coral, red with indignation. "Bertram doesn't deserve to be —"

"I meant the knight," said Thomas.

"Are you suggesting that . . . no, it wouldn't be right!" said Romaric, appalled.

"Look, enough of this arguing," replied Thomas, getting to his feet. "Robin's life could be in danger and all you're doing is bickering about what to do!"

"He's right. Let's go!" shouted Amber. "Thomas, I'm with you."

"Hey, Amber, cool it!" Romaric tried to calm her down. "The minute anyone says Robin's name, you go completely crazy."

"No. They're right, Romaric. What are we waiting for?" asked Agatha, leaping to her feet.

"Yes, let's get the knight!" echoed Bertram, joining them, thrilled that nobody was asking him to cast a spell anymore.

The four reckless friends leaped out from behind the rock and rushed yelling toward the poor knight, who couldn't believe his eyes. He watched them come racing toward him in open-mouthed amazement, wondering what sort of game these children were playing.

"Come on," said Romaric to Godfrey and Coral. "We have no choice; we'll have to go and help those idiots."

"Why don't we yell, too?" asked Coral.

"Because . . . well . . . oh, go on then, yell if it makes you happy," replied Romaric, at a loss.

"YAHAAAAAA!"

The astonished knight was caught unawares when the seven youngsters ran straight at him. And when they grabbed his legs he just keeled over. He hadn't had the presence of mind to defend himself.

"I've got his right leg!" shouted Bertram when their victim was lying on the ground.

"And I've got the left!" cried Godfrey.

"I've got his arm!" said Romaric.

"I've got the other one!" said Coral.

Thomas was sitting firmly on the man's back.

"But what on earth . . . what . . . ?" was all the knight could say. He was easily old enough to be their father.

Eventually, Amber pulled out a rope and a sock from her backpack. With Agatha's help, she bound the knight and gagged him with the sock.

"There's no need to make a face; it's clean!" Amber reassured him.

Then they abandoned the poor knight, telling him they'd be back later, and went up to The Door to The Uncertain World.

"If Bertram fails, we've had it. We won't be able to do anything," Agatha groaned.

"We could always try and apologize to that poor knight . . . ," retorted Romaric.

"Oh, that's enough!" snapped Amber. "You know we had no choice."

"Shut up!" said Coral. "Bertram needs silence to concentrate. If he does manage to open The Door, I'd like us to stay together this time."

Bertram walked right up to the monumental Door that led to The Uncertain World. Like the one that led to The Real World, it was very high and very wide. Hundreds of Graphems were carved into the oak panels. With a trembling hand, the sorcerer tentatively touched the signs. But to his great surprise they were warm, and immediately began to glow, for though he didn't know it, a few hours earlier two hundred knights had passed through The Door, and that had made it easy to reactivate the opening spell. Bertram felt a huge sense of relief. He turned to his companions and announced with newfound assurance:

"I think it's going to be fine."

10

THE HOWLING COAST

T he Knights of the Brotherhood's passage between the two
Worlds went without a hitch. The men, unaccustomed to
magic, had conducted themselves bravely, but they were hugely
relieved to set foot on solid ground when they landed on The
Middle Island. Gerald and Qadwan were drained from their
efforts — opening The Door to The Uncertain World, and then
holding it open, had required considerable energy. So they
stopped for a rest and the Commander took the opportunity to
explain to his men precisely what was at stake.

Anxious to avoid any leaks that could have alerted The Shadow's
spies on The Lost Isle, the Provost had asked the Commander to
maintain the utmost secrecy, and so the knights were unaware
that Robin had been kidnapped. When they learned of it from
the lips of their chief, they reacted indignantly.

"Attacking a child!" groaned one.

"And not just any child!" added Bertolen, who had once let

Robin jump up behind him on his horse and had taken him to Bromotul to visit Romaric. "If I get my hands on The Shadow, I'll make him sorry."

"What are we waiting for?" cried Ambor, visibly simmering with impatience. "Let's go and rescue Robin from the clutches of that devil!"

"Knights, I understand your anger," replied the Commander, raising his hand in a calming gesture. "But we must remain cool-headed. Right now we are in a dangerous world where The Shadow is very powerful. Let's not get carried away. We will only succeed in helping Robin if we remain calm."

"The Commander is right," agreed Gerald, who had joined them. "Especially since we don't even know where to begin looking for Robin," he added anxiously.

"So what are we going to do?" Bertolen asked the sorcerer.

"First of all, we must get off this island," replied Gerald.

"I'll take care of that," said the Commander. "Ambor, Bertolen, with me! You others, be ready to leave."

The Middle Island was like a huge water lily. Flat and rocky, windswept and battered by the waves, it should have been deserted. But a small community of fishermen lived there, most of them in an unfortified village. The island was safe from Gommons and other sea monsters because the surrounding ocean was infested with Stingers, huge jellyfish that Romaric had once just managed to escape. In the absence of any vegetation on land, the fishermen lived on the abundant produce of the sea: seaweed and plentiful supplies of fish.

While the men got ready for departure, the Commander

set off for the village to negotiate their transportation to the mainland.

Gerald went back to Qadwan, who was finding it difficult to move.

"Ouch!" winced the elderly sorcerer. "I'm too old for all this!"

"I'd never have gotten all those knights here without you," Gerald said gratefully, placing an affectionate hand on his shoulder.

"To thank me, you can send me on a vacation to the Purple Mountains!" joked Qadwan.

"And leave those unruly apprentices to run riot in your gym?"

"By the spirits of Gifdu, of course not!" he growled. "Give me a few more minutes and I'll join you."

"Of course. Give yourself time to recover. In any case, I need to make contact with Quadehar. How clever of him to think of coming here with Valentino and Urian . . . for this mission we need all the help we can get, his especially!"

Gerald closed his eyes and wove a mental communication spell based on Berkana, taking care to call on the Graphems in their Uncertain form. Still tired from his efforts to open The Door, it was hard for him to reach Master Quadehar, who couldn't believe his ears when he recognized Gerald's voice. His sorcerer friend gave him a quick outline of the situation and told him of Robin's disappearance.

Quadehar's voice betrayed none of his anger and concern. With his usual composure, he offered to join the army of knights, together with Urian and Valentino, and to pool their resources.

Gerald was relieved to know that the Guild's most powerful

sorcerer would soon be at his side; The Uncertain World was no laughing matter. Quadehar and his two companions were already on the Russet Heath, and they decided to meet up in the hills above the Howling Coast.

Shortly afterward, the Commander returned with some good news: In exchange for a handful of precious stones — which the knights had fortunately brought with them in large quantities — the fishermen had agreed to place all the boats they required at the disposal of the army that had appeared out of the blue.

As soon as all the men and equipment were aboard the twenty or so large vessels, the turquoise armada set sail.

The crossing was uneventful, other than for the appearance of a shoal of Stingers which had the knights in a panic, for they were unfamiliar with the ocean world and its dangers. Gerald had wondered why The Lost Isle had never had a navy. But now the answer was glaringly obvious — quite simply because no enemy had ever dared to travel across the treacherous ocean from which The Lost Isle rose in isolated splendor.

After what felt to the knights like an eternity, they at last disembarked at the northwestern tip of the Howling Coast. Led by the two sorcerers, the two hundred knights set off eastward in marching formation, glad to leave the shore behind them. The strong, icy wind restored their good humor; it reminded them of home, where they were used to the bracing winds of the moors.

They stopped to rest in a little valley. Gerald talked to them about The Uncertain World while they tucked into their rations of bread. They set off again and marched steadily for most of the afternoon, keeping their spirits up by singing songs from The Lost Isle.

Qadwan was the first to spot the smoke from a fire in the distance.

"That must be Quadehar," Gerald said to the Commander.

Not wanting to take any risks, they decided to wait and send some scouts ahead. They were soon back.

"Three men, two wearing the armor of the Brotherhood and one sporting the cloak of the Guild," announced the commando leader. "Sitting around a fire. Rocky terrain, deserted."

"Quadehar, Urian, and Valentino!" exclaimed Gerald delightedly. "Everything is fine, Commander!"

A few moments later, the army from The Lost Isle marched up to the three men. It was a joyful reunion. Urian Penmarch slapped the veterans heartily on the shoulder and pinched the cheeks of the younger knights, booming with laughter. Valentino gripped the hand of the Commander, who had been his fencing pupil at Bromotul, and an emotional Quadehar embraced his two fellow sorcerers from Gifdu.

"Thank you, thank you, my friends, for having gotten here so quickly. With the help of the knights, we have a good chance of saving Robin."

Gerald flashed him a reassuring smile. But he knew Quadehar well, and he could see how concerned the sorcerer was for the safety of his apprentice.

"We'll camp here tonight," declared the Commander. "Ambor, organize the watch. Bertolen, tell the men to pitch camp. Then both of you join me by the fire with our friends."

Each man had brought with him a piece of canvas which formed a section of a tent, and the knights' camp was soon set up. Vigilant guards kept watch on all sides.

The Commander, Urian and Valentino, Ambor and Bertolen, and the three sorcerers met around the fire at the center of the camp. Bertolen passed around a gourd filled with sweet wine, which they all sipped in turn.

"Let me introduce Ambor and Bertolen, the most valiant of my knights," said the Commander, pointing to the pair. "They will be my captains during this campaign. Urian and Valentino need no introduction. Everybody in the Brotherhood has heard of the legendary Don Quixote and Sancho Panza!"

They all burst out laughing, and Urian and Valentino chuckled on hearing their nicknames from the days when they'd been active knights.

"Now," went on the Commander, "let's get down to business. Quadehar, Gerald, Qadwan, we're all ears."

Quadehar sat silent, deep in thought. Gerald cleared his throat and spoke:

"Robin was kidnapped just outside Penmarch by someone who is practiced in the art of magic and who was masquerading as my pupil, Bertram. Everything suggests that it was one of The Shadow's henchmen — if not The Shadow himself. I petitioned the Provost to embark on this operation, which is unparalleled in the history of The Lost Isle, because I have a premonition of great danger. A great danger for Robin. And a great danger for us all."

The sorcerer's words were greeted with silence. Nobody doubted that Robin was at risk — after all, The Shadow had tried to snatch the boy on several occasions. And if such an evil creature wanted him so badly, there must be a very good reason. Each person, even Urian, knew in his heart that their fate and that of the young apprentice — and perhaps the future of the whole Lost Isle — were inextricably linked.

"Well, at least we can be thankful that Robin's friends aren't mixed up in this," said Valentino.

"I made sure that they will stay quietly at home and mind their own business," confirmed Gerald smugly. "Those kids are capable of getting themselves into the most unbelievable predicaments!"

≋ ✳ ≋ ✳ ≋

"Now what?" Agatha asked, surveying their surroundings. The friends had just emerged into The Uncertain World.

"Now we have to find somewhere to spend the night," replied Romaric, supporting Bertram.

The young sorcerer was exhausted by the effort of opening the magic Door.

"There are houses over there, down by the water," Godfrey pointed out.

"Probably fishermen's cottages," said Romaric. "Let's head there. Bertram desperately needs to rest."

"Mmm, I've seen him look better," added Coral teasingly.

"If that's all the thanks I get, next time you can make do without me," grumbled Bertram feebly.

The little gang set off toward the village that Godfrey had spotted.

They were greeted by a few fishermen who were rather suspicious of them at first. But when they realized the strangers were only children, they relaxed. The women, however, couldn't help making snide comments about mothers who allowed their offspring to roam all over the place. All the same, they rustled up a delicious meal of fish and shellfish.

"I've never seen so many people come through The Door," said a fisherman, spitting on the floor.

He was small and wiry, and seemed to be the village chief.

"And you've never earned so many precious stones before!" retorted another man cheerily.

The fisherman chuckled.

"Do you mean that other people from The Lost Isle arrived here before us?" asked Romaric in surprise.

"I don't know where they came from, but there were a hell of a lot of them. Around two hundred. And they weren't exactly light, either, with all that armor on!"

The other fishermen chortled.

"Terrific!" enthused Coral. "That means that Gerald managed to convince the Provost. The Knights of the Wind are here in The Uncertain World and they're going to rescue Robin!"

"I'm sure you're right," said Amber, who despite everything seemed slightly disappointed. "I mean, it's great. . . ."

She didn't sound convinced.

They had responded eagerly to Romaric's suggestion, certain that nobody else would go to Robin's aid. They had felt it their duty to do so. But two hundred knights led by a Master Sorcerer had beaten them to it, making their attempt look pathetic.

"What should we do now?" asked Thomas.

"There are two options," Amber pointed out. "Either we go

straight back to The Lost Isle and leave the knights to sort this out, or we try to help them."

"Since we're here, we might as well stay and try and help," suggested Romaric.

"I agree," said Godfrey, while the others muttered their approval. "But what use can we be to the knights?"

Amber had a word with the village chief, then turned to the others.

"They've got a day's head start. Let's wait until tomorrow before asking Bertram to contact Gerald telepathically. We'll see what he has to say."

"In any case, Bertram is quite incapable of opening The Door again or communicating mentally with anyone tonight," said Agatha, jerking her head in the direction of the young sorcerer, who had fallen asleep in a corner of the little room they had been lent for the night.

"And supposing Gerald blows his top?" fretted Coral.

"We'll pretend there's interference on the magic 'phone' line and that we can't hear him very well, then we'll cut him off," said Amber calmly. "We can always carry on by ourselves. Like the rest of you, I think that the presence of the knights in The Uncertain World is terrific news. But something tells me that this is not going to be easy. . . ."

"You're right," said Thomas. "You four know The Uncertain World better than Gerald or any of the knights. Robin might need your experience just as much as the strength of the Brotherhood."

"You know, you're not so dumb," said Amber to the red-headed boy, giving him an affectionate prod. "Especially as the fisherman I spoke to has agreed to take us on his boat to the spot where he dropped the men of the Brotherhood, for the price of a few precious stones."

Amber's suggestion was put to the vote. They were all for it, except Bertram, who was in a deep sleep.

11

FIRST BATTLE

Robin had tried to keep track of time, but had eventually given up. The light filtering in through the skylight was too feeble for him to be able to tell whether it was from the sun, or artificial. The apprentice sorcerer wasn't completely in the dark, however: The blue glow from the walls of his cleverly modified Armor of Egishjamur, and the red-tinged flames coming from the branches of Hagal bathed the cell in a soft, ghostly light. For a while, Robin almost felt reassured: The glow meant that the spell was working.

But anxiety was gradually getting the better of him, and he started to imagine all the possible scenarios. The Shadow was bound to unleash his infinite magic powers against him. Or perhaps just keep him there forever . . . even if The Shadow was unable to break through his defenses, what was there to stop him from starving Robin to death, as armies did when they besieged a town?

But Robin had a hunch that The Shadow would be incapable

of waiting. He had tried to picture his enemy but had only managed to conjure up a hazy form of indeterminate shape. Without knowing why, Robin guessed that his foe was impatient. He was convinced of it. And so he was only mildly surprised when The Shadow entered the room.

At first, Robin couldn't see anything. He merely heard the door open and close again. The fuzzy walls of his magic rampart prevented him from seeing clearly. Then he noticed something very close to him, on the other side of the Armor of Egishjamur. A shadow. A dark patch of shadow in the half-dark room, from which the light seemed to flee.

A terrifying whisper sent a chill down his spine:

"Welcome . . . boy . . . my dear boy . . ."

It was a hollow, powerful voice. At first, Robin stood there petrified. He had to muster up all his courage to answer:

"Are you . . . are you The Shadow?"

The dark silhouette cackled. Robin saw that it had moved. It seemed to be floating. The Shadow was circling Robin's magic protection, looking for a chink in his defenses.

"That's what I'm known as . . . where you come from. . . ."

Robin watched The Shadow groping his way along the translucent wall. In the places he touched, the light became less intense. A wave of panic swept over Robin.

"What do you want?"

He had shouted. The Shadow froze for a whole second. He seemed pleased.

"Well . . . well . . . you are afraid. . . . Perhaps I should not have wasted my time against your spells. . . ."

The Shadow withdrew. Robin's vision became oddly blurred

and he could no longer see him, but he was still there. Robin could sense his evil presence in the same way that one can feel the damp, or when a room feels stuffy. He couldn't help starting when he heard The Shadow's voice again.

"My dear boy . . . why should we fight? Trust me. . . ."

"You attacked my country! You killed people! You kidnapped me!"

Robin was shouting again. He felt as though if he tried to speak in a normal voice, his words would be muffled.

"Tut, tut . . . ," murmured The Shadow reasonably. "Those are mere details. You don't know what I have to offer you. . . ."

"I don't want anything from you. You disgust me!"

"Come . . . my dear boy. I'm offering you the three Worlds on a plate. . . ."

"Shut up! Shut up!"

Robin crouched down and covered his ears with both hands to shut out the voice that was insinuating itself inside him and chilling him to the bone.

"Why are you afraid of me? I'm offering you power . . . a partnership . . ."

In a final attempt to block out The Shadow's voice, Robin shouted:

"Never! Never! I hate you! You're a devil! I despise you!"

That seemed to touch a raw nerve. The Shadow advanced and, in a fit of anger, hurled a ball of gray flames against the Armor. The ball, filled with evil magic, shattered against the wall of energy and began to fizzle. Curiously, this unexpected attack frightened Robin less than the measured tones of The Shadow's hollow voice.

"Young fool . . . don't provoke me . . . and never insult me again. Come what may . . . you will be mine. As an ally . . . or as a slave. Think about my offer. Think carefully. I'll be back soon. . . ."

The door opened and closed again. The Shadow had left.

Robin closed his eyes and tried to still his pounding heart. He was trembling from top to toe. He had never been so frightened in his life. The Shadow oozed power. Robin realized that his own determination was crucial to countering The Shadow's evil designs: If he hadn't resisted, The Shadow would have swept aside his defenses and forced him to do his will. But Robin knew that he wouldn't have the strength to hold out indefinitely. . . . He huddled up and burst into tears of despair.

Giving vent to his misery made him feel better; gradually, the fear and panic subsided and Robin's spirits were revived. He sat up and took a sip of water. Then he went over to the spot where the ball of shadows had hit the Armor of Egishjamur.

He frowned and carefully inspected the remaining shreds of darkness. On impact with the magic wall they had fizzled and slowly disintegrated.

He could not believe what he saw at first, and it filled him with hope: His wall was intact! Nothing, not a scratch! Which meant that . . . Robin went back over what had happened. The Shadow had walked all around the Armor and tested its resistance. Then he had suggested they become partners. It was not out of generosity that The Shadow had made that offer; it was because he was not certain he could demolish Robin's defenses. The Shadow had almost persuaded him to surrender. . . . But, in losing his temper and hurling that spell at Robin that hadn't worked, The Shadow had shown that he was not invincible, and that all was not yet lost.

Reassured a little, Robin went back and sat down on Mannaz, feeling almost pleased with himself.

12

THE HAUNTED FOREST

At dawn, Robin's friends had awoken cold and hungry. It had taken them a moment to remember that they were in a fishing village on The Middle Island in The Uncertain World, and it had taken them even longer to crawl out of their sleeping bags. Now, perched on the rocks beside the water, they started on their food supplies. Bertram felt rested and had more color in his cheeks than the night before. But when he tried to contact Gerald using a communication spell, his head began to throb so violently that he wasn't able to do any magic.

"It doesn't matter," said Amber. "In any case we've got Plan B, which means we take the initiative."

After breakfast, the kind fisherman who had offered to ferry them over to the Howling Coast in his boat dropped them off at the spot where the knights had disembarked the day before.

The Howling Coast owed its name to the many Gommons, those nasty creatures resembling humans, with hair of seaweed and scaly skin, that roamed its shores. On stormy nights their terrifying howls could be heard above the roar of the waves.

Agatha paid the fisherman with the precious stones she had found at her parents' place. Then they left the shore as fast as they could.

The knights had left a visible trail.

"Following them will be a piece of cake," muttered Thomas.

His father was a hunter and he knew about tracking.

They studied the map of The Uncertain World, which Amber had fished out of her bag. She had copied it from Robin's the previous summer and had had the presence of mind to bring it along when she left Krakal for Dashtikazar. It was clear that the knights were heading due south.

The friends set off across the russet grasses of the heath, which rustled and crunched underfoot.

"Do you think that Quadehar will be furious with us?" asked Coral, walking beside Godfrey.

"Quadehar? I don't think so. But Gerald will be, for certain," he replied quietly.

While everyone thought Quadehar was still a prisoner at Gifdu, Bertram had informed them that he was in The Uncertain World with Urian Penmarch and Valentino. Bertram was convinced that Gerald and the knights, newly arrived from The Lost Isle, would contact Quadehar straight away and join him. This information had both reassured them and given them cause for concern.

At lunchtime, they decided to stop for something to eat. Bertram sank down on to the ground.

"Aaagh!" he groaned. "I can't stop thinking about Gerald.

I hope he won't be too angry with me when he finds out we're here."

"No wonder you're feeling guilty," said Coral. "He gave you the job of keeping us on The Lost Isle, and here we are in The Uncertain World."

"Thanks for the moral support, Coral!" replied Bertram.

"What about me? Don't I get any sympathy?" asked Romaric.

"My valiant squire!" exclaimed Coral.

"That's precisely the problem," he said, momentarily thrown by Coral's teasing and the others' laughter. "I am indeed a squire. And I've run away from Bromotul. I . . . I assaulted — there's no other word for it — a knight near The Door. And now I'm chasing after the very people that common sense tells me I should avoid at all costs — my uncle and half of the Brotherhood! How do you think I feel?"

"Well, it can't get much worse," sympathized Amber.

"Other than being called 'my valiant squire' by a girl in front of two hundred knights!" teased Godfrey.

"Shut up!" snapped Coral. "You're just jealous."

"Well, I'd love to be called someone's valiant something-or-other," confessed Thomas ruefully.

"You see, Godfrey?" Coral said triumphantly. "Some boys know how to be romantic!"

"And some girls have no sense," sighed Amber. "Let's keep up our strength. We've still got a long trek ahead of us. We need to keep calm."

〰 ✳ 〰 ✳ 〰

As evening fell, the sorcerers and knights reached the fringes of a wild-looking forest that gave them goosebumps and made their hearts quicken with apprehension.

"The Haunted Forest," announced Master Quadehar.

His friends gathered around the map he was studying.

"You're right," confirmed Urian. "There's The Middle Island, the Howling Coast where we landed, and the Russet Heath which we've just crossed."

After a short halt, they entered the wood behind the scouts, glancing warily about them.

The trees were not very tall, but their trunks were thick and covered with gray moss, and beneath their dense foliage the branches were twisted like tentacles.

"Brrr! I can think of more pleasant places," commented Urian.

Valentino turned to him. "But there's no better place to conceal an army!" he said with a wink.

They soon came into a glade where the ground was covered with a strange tawny grass. After consulting Gerald and Quadehar, the Commander gave the order to pitch camp.

Once they were all sitting comfortably around one of the fires, the knights' leader spoke to the sorcerers:

"Master Sorcerers, what are your plans now?"

"First of all, we have to get closer to the inhabited regions of The Uncertain World and find a sheltered position," replied Quadehar, stretching his legs. "We were too vulnerable and, above all, too far away from habitation on the Howling Coast."

"Does that mean we're going to stay here?" asked Valentino.

"Until we find out where Robin has been taken," replied Gerald.

"This forest is dense, and nobody ventures here of their own free will," continued Quadehar. "People say that in the old days, the priests of Yenibohor used to hang their enemies in this forest. Nowadays, everybody believes it's haunted by the ghosts of all those who were murdered."

"Ghosts?" echoed Urian anxiously.

"Don't tell me you're afraid of ghosts!" taunted Qadwan, leaning up against a tree for support.

"No, er . . . of course not! But why wait? Give me fifty men," he thundered, "and within three days I'll get the information we need out of the thugs who inhabit The Uncertain World!"

"That's precisely the sort of tactic that ends in disaster," Quadehar rebuked him. "The more discreet we are, the better our chances. . . ."

"Is it The Shadow you're afraid of?" asked the Commander. "I fought him once, on The Lost Isle, in the Golden Mountains. And my knights and I defeated him."

"Things are different in The Uncertain World," explained Quadehar. "Without going into detail, magic doesn't work in the same way as it does back home. Perhaps that's why The Shadow is much more powerful here than on The Lost Isle. I have never had the opportunity to meet him until now. But had I done so, I probably wouldn't have been any match for him."

This admission by the most powerful sorcerer in the Guild plunged the men sitting around the fire into an awkward silence. If he was no match for The Shadow, what chance would there be for them?

"Let's get straight to the point," suggested Valentino. "What's the best way to find Robin?"

"We thought we'd be able to locate him using a spell," replied

Gerald. "But sadly we haven't been able to. His abductor seems to have thought of everything."

"I fear we'll have to resign ourselves to using more traditional methods, such as sending spies into the main cities to glean any information that might lead us to Robin," continued Quadehar glumly.

"But time is of the essence," said Gerald.

"I know. But I don't see any other solu —"

Quadehar was cut short by a tremendous uproar. There was fighting in the woods, close to the glade.

They all leaped to their feet.

"The ghosts!" groaned Urian. "The ghosts are here!"

"Shut up, for goodness' sake!" scolded Valentino. "Can't you see that it's just an intruder?"

The din had indeed stopped and, assisted by the knights who had rushed to their aid, the sentries at the northwest of the clearing were coming toward them, keeping a firm grip on a man who wasn't even attempting to escape.

A tall, sturdy man, wearing a voluminous red cloak . . .

One of the guards pulled down the prisoner's hood.

"Yorwan!" exclaimed Master Quadehar, catching sight of the familiar face.

"Yorwan?" roared Urian, rushing at him with clenched fists. "By Jove, I swear I'll beat the living daylights out of you!"

"Commander!" shouted Quadehar. "Restrain Urian!"

In a flash, the Commander stepped between the prisoner and the enraged veteran knight.

"Let me go!" bellowed Urian, struggling.

The Commander had difficulty holding him back.

"Let me give that traitor his just deserts!" roared Urian, in a fury.

Ambor and Bertolen raced over to help their chief control him.

Quadehar's shouts, then those of Urian, had roused the knights, who also had painful memories of Yorwan's treachery. An old wound had been reopened. Quadehar, on the other hand, felt full of hope. To calm everyone down, he clambered up onto a fallen tree trunk and demanded silence:

"Listen to me! Urian is right! This man, who in The Uncertain World is known as Lord Sha, is indeed Yorwan, the treacherous sorcerer who stole the *Book of the Stars* in his youth. And of course he should be condemned for that, but this is neither the time nor the place. Yorwan obviously came looking for us. He offered no resistance when we captured him, even though he is a perfect master of the magic of this world. I think he has a good reason for acting thus. Let's leave aside our resentment and listen to the important news he has to tell us."

The Master Sorcerer's arguments swayed the men, and even Urian calmed down as he prepared, along with the others, to listen carefully to what their prisoner had to say.

"I know where Robin is," said Lord Sha quite simply.

≈ ✳ ≈ ✳ ≈

Robin's friends decided to spend the night on the heath. It reminded them of the moors around Dashtikazar where they liked to roam on summer evenings. They weren't daunted by the strangeness of this world or the large, weird, catlike creatures they had glimpsed several times during the day, nor were they afraid of being alone in the middle of nowhere.

They gathered as many twigs as they could and lit a fire. Then they sat down and devoured the provisions they had saved up.

"The tracks we're following are more and more recent," declared Thomas. "We should catch up with Gerald tomorrow. . . ."

"Thank goodness," said Coral. "We haven't got much food left! Apart from a few cans . . ."

"Now you know what it's like to go hungry, Coral," teased Godfrey. "So you're prepared to sacrifice the heady taste of freedom for the satisfaction of your stomach!"

"I'll sacrifice you if you carry on like that!" protested Coral, peeved. "If there isn't much to eat, that tall, skinny body of yours might start to look tempting!"

"It reminds me of a fable I heard in The Real World," said Bertram wistfully. "Do you study Aesop's fables at school?"

"Do you think we're ignoramuses or what?" replied Agatha.

"It's the fable of the Wolf and the Dog," continued Bertram. "The wolf, who's starving, envies the life of the dog, who is always well fed. His new friend persuades him to turn himself into a dog. But when he finds out that he can no longer run free, he's off . . ."

". . . saying 'better starve free than be a fat slave,'" finished Amber. "Yes, I know it, it's a lovely story. . . ."

The friends gazed into the fire for a moment without speaking. They all understood the wolf's cruel dilemma as they felt their stomachs rumble.

13

THE SHADOWS ARE
UNLEASHED

Robin opened his eyes abruptly, his heart hammering wildly. He glanced around the room, and then peered more closely into the dark corners, but couldn't see a thing. He tried to calm down. He'd been asleep but he was sure he'd heard the cell door open.

How many times had he been startled into consciousness like this, emerging breathless from a deep sleep, like a drowning person desperately trying to swim to the surface? The waiting was driving him crazy.

"So, boy . . ."

Robin nearly jumped out of his skin and cried out. The Shadow! The Shadow was there in the room. So he hadn't been dreaming. He was as tense as a bowstring, unable to relax, even in his sleep. How long was it since he had eaten? Days? A week, maybe . . .

"Tut, tut . . . You're jumpy . . . much too jumpy. . . ."

The hollow whispering was moving around the room. At last Robin could make out the shadowy silhouette on the other side of the Armor of Egishjamur. He could barely distinguish it, but he could hear it breathing, and he thought he could feel an icy breath on his face. Robin began to tremble like a leaf.

"Well, boy . . ." The icy whisper sounded very close. "Have you thought . . . about my offer . . . ?"

Robin did not reply at once. Come on! He absolutely must get a grip and stop shaking. He closed his eyes and asked, almost praying, for the help of Isaz, the Graphem that helped concentration and strengthened the will. Deep down inside him, Isaz glowed and spread its warmth throughout his body.

When Robin looked at The Shadow again, he wasn't trembling so badly.

"I've thought about it. The answer is NO."

The Shadow seemed to grow, the darkness around him intensifying as he hissed, "You dare say no to me . . . to me . . . ?"

He drew back and gave a terrifying roar.

"Very well. It's your decision. You don't want to be my ally, so you shall be my slave."

Robin knew that a confrontation was inevitable. He glanced rapidly around to ensure that his defenses were still intact, and hurriedly sat down on Mannaz.

Out of the darkness, The Shadow produced a dark ball of flames like the one he had thrown during his previous visit, and hurled it violently against the magic wall.

The spell shattered against the Armor of Egishjamur. Like the previous time, it began to sizzle.

The Shadow threw another ball, and again it failed to penetrate Robin's protection.

"Why does he keep on?" wondered Robin anxiously. "He can see that these weapons aren't powerful enough to smash my Armor."

His gaze was drawn to the floor. He noticed that the Egishjamur drawn on the flagstones were glowing intensely. The dark flames were mobilizing all their energy! And while the Egishjamur were fighting against them, *they couldn't repel an attack from a different source*! Robin's eyes opened wide. He had just realized what The Shadow was up to. He tried to reassure himself by passing his hands over the red flames of Hagal.

When about twenty evil balls of flame were clinging to the walls of the Galdr, The Shadow confidently advanced toward Robin. He touched the Armor and thrust an arm through, as if plunging it into water. He laughed triumphantly and tried to break through the wall of energy.

At the same time, the Odala Graphems, which Robin had drawn between each Egishjamur to reinforce the wall, began to glow. The arm that The Shadow had poked through the magic barrier was suddenly attacked by myriad burning sparks. He groaned in pain.

"A double protection! Bravo, my boy. . . . I expected no less. I'm certainly not disappointed in you. . . ."

The shadowy figure chanted a spell in a tongue that Robin

had never heard. The sparks gradually died away as the spell grew louder and more powerful.

"*Pon choktu gher na gher noa magar gudaz bashzir noa . . .*"

The signs of Odala on the ground stopped glowing. With an anguished howl, The Shadow broke through the Armor of Egishjamur. Robin stifled a scream. The enemy had forced his way inside his walls and was besieging him in his keep!

But The Shadow had barely overcome the Galdr when a red halo began to glow around the giant Graphem of Hagal, whose eight branches crackled with a cold fire, placing Robin under the protection of a new wall of energy.

The Shadow froze, caught off guard by this new spell.

"I underestimated you, my boy. . . . We all misjudged you," he whispered menacingly.

He tapped the transparent barrier that separated him from the boy. He was very close and Robin could make out a vaguely human form beneath the gray cloak. Without being able to say why, he suddenly felt less afraid.

"Impressive . . . very impressive . . ."

The Shadow forced himself against the red wall and stretched out his arm. A black cloak plunged Robin into darkness; he instinctively huddled up. With a mighty roar, The Shadow called upon all the powers of The Uncertain World. And the evil spirits were unleashed . . .

Never had Robin witnessed such a display of magic. Ghostly figures with hazy forms appeared out of thin air and tried to batter the keep of Hagal, screeching with rage as they attacked again and again. The Shadow urged them on in a terrifying voice. Robin began to scream. With fright. With madness, perhaps.

Until the protection of Hagal cracked, fissured, and caved in amid a burst of red stars.

The Shadow staggered, groaning with relief. The specters melted away as mysteriously as they had appeared. Visibly exhausted by his efforts, The Shadow slowly approached a sobbing Robin.

"Now you are mine. You are mine, my boy. . . ."

The Shadow stretched out his arm to grab him.

The ground beneath Robin trembled slightly. Mannaz had sprung into action. In a fraction of a second the Graphem enveloped Robin in a milky white light that formed the shape of a giant sphere. The cosmic sphere. The ultimate refuge.

The Shadow stopped dead. He hesitated, then reeled backward. Robin saw all this through his tears and realized that he no longer had anything to fear: The Shadow had used up all his powers against Egishjamur, Odala, and Hagal. He had no energy left to attack Mannaz.

The door to the cell suddenly swung open and a shaved-headed man dressed in a light-colored tunic came into the room. He stopped in his tracks when he caught sight of Robin, then bowed low before The Shadow.

"Master . . . excuse me, Master, but . . . a foreign army is camped outside the city gates."

The Shadow repressed an angry gesture.

"Already! They are here already? You bring me bad news, Lomgo. Too soon . . . it is too soon."

Then he turned to Robin and said coldly:

"It seems I have to leave you, but I haven't finished with you yet. I have other means . . . yes, other means. . . ."

The Shadow left the room cursing, followed by Lomgo, who walked with stooped shoulders, his head lolling to one side.

Robin tried to fight against the buzzing in his head, but it was futile. Exhausted by all the emotion and weak from hunger, he lost consciousness once again.

14

YENIBOHOR

"What do we do now?" asked Bertram.

Bemused, the friends gazed at the forbidding walls of the city of Yenibohor looming in the distance. It was the first time they had set eyes on the famous town, and they were awestruck. Yenibohor was shrouded in an atmosphere of terror and dread. A giant tower rose up in the center of the city, heightening the sense of menace.

"So this is the haunt of the priests who terrorize everyone!" exclaimed Godfrey, neatly avoiding Bertram's question.

"Wal, the Keeper of the Salvaged Objects of the People of the Sea, told me terrible stories about them," said Coral.

"And the stories are all true," confirmed Romaric, looking glum.

During his last trip to The Uncertain World, Romaric had met some men who had warned him about the priests of Yenibohor.

"We definitely have a knack for getting ourselves into hot water," Agatha sighed.

"But you have to admit that for the time being, all we've done is follow the knights," snapped Amber. "It's not our fault if they led us here!"

It was true that Robin's friends had simply followed the footsteps of the Brotherhood across the Russet Heath. And they had finally come across the knights in battle formation outside the walls of Yenibohor. They all agreed it might be best to put off the moment of the joyful reunion and . . . the explanations. They were in no hurry. There are times when hiding out in the woods with the wolves can seem like the better option.

So they made for high ground and a rocky outcrop not far from the city, called The Gray Hills. This vantage point gave them a good view of the knights' preparations from a safe distance.

"Well, okay. Now what do we do?" repeated Bertram.

"We do what they're doing, down on the plain," replied Romaric without hesitating. "We wait. . . ."

≈ ✳ ≈ ✳ ≈

In an attitude that was both heroic and almost ridiculous given the circumstances, the ranks of turquoise breastplates stood openly before the gates of the powerful city of Yenibohor. At the rear, studying a rough plan of the city, the Commander was holding a council of war with Ambor, Bertolen, Urian, and Valentino.

"Commander," Urian Penmarch repeated for the tenth time, "I don't understand why you're allowing that traitor Yorwan to take charge of the operation!"

Valentino gave a sigh of exasperation.

"That's because you've made up your mind not to understand," he replied, taking the place of the knights' leader. "Urian, please . . . first of all, get it into your head that Yorwan's not in charge of anything. He is giving us information, that's all. What he might have done in the past is one thing, but what he's doing today is helping us to find Robin."

"Are you suggesting that one good deed will wipe out his past crimes?" exclaimed Ambor. "That's out of the question!"

"That's not even the issue," complained Urian. "It's not a good deed, but a trap. And we're rushing headlong into it. If Yorwan weren't under the protection of those wretched sorcerers, I'd have strangled him with my own hands to stop him from doing any more damage!"

"May I remind you, we are here to organize the storming of the city," the Commander cut in harshly. "So let's put our minds to that instead of indulging in pointless speculation. Yorwan claims that Robin is being held prisoner here in Yenibohor. If Quadehar and Gerald tell us that we can trust Yorwan's information, then it is because it's reliable. It's not up to us to judge. . . ."

Urian didn't reply, but clenched his fists until his knuckles turned white.

Some distance away, Quadehar, Gerald, and Qadwan sat in the short grass around Yorwan, who was enveloped in the red cloak of Lord Sha. Watching them chatting freely and amicably, nobody could have imagined that one of the men was the prisoner of the other three.

"I can't believe that I missed my apprentice's cry for help," lamented Quadehar.

"It's because you are less sensitive than I am to the Graphems of The Uncertain World," replied Yorwan.

"But I did hear him," insisted the Master Sorcerer. "Faintly, but I definitely recognized it as a cry for help. Only it came from The Uncertain World. How could I have known it was from Robin?"

He was furious with himself for not having paid more attention to the random spell he had intercepted when walking toward Virdu a few days earlier.

"The main thing is that Yorwan picked up the call, and above all, that he had the presence of mind to locate Robin and start tailing him telepathically," Gerald consoled him.

"I lost track of him in Yenibohor," continued Yorwan. "I think he must still be here. But . . ."

"But what?" asked Qadwan wearily.

The old sorcerer was still weak. The journey to The Uncertain World had exhausted him.

"But we must be extremely vigilant," continued Yorwan. "The priests of Yenibohor are very powerful. They practice an evil strain of magic based on the worship of Bohor, the Master of Darkness. People say that the High Priest does not have a human form, and that he was sent to The Uncertain World by Bohor himself. . . . In any case, we must proceed with great caution."

He glanced disapprovingly at the knights stationed conspicuously outside the city.

Qadwan sighed.

"That's the Brotherhood all over, proud and unreasonable. You just have to accept that. But the knights are brave. They are unequaled, in any world!"

"The knights haven't got a hope against the priests," insisted Yorwan.

"What do you suggest?" asked Quadehar.

"Guile or negotiation. Certainly not force."

"I know I'm repeating myself, but we have very little time," said Gerald. "Whoever kidnapped Robin — The Shadow, High Priest, or Bohor himself — he'll soon get what he wants out of him. And what's more, if it is the same person who stole the *Book of the Stars* from the Tower, as you told us, then you can be sure that something terrible is going to happen. . . ."

"You must believe me," implored Yorwan. "*The Book of the Stars* was stolen from my tower at Jaghatel while I was pursuing Robin along the corridors of Gifdu."

"A robber robbed! Now, that would be funny if the situation weren't so dramatic," Qadwan blurted out.

Yorwan gazed dejectedly at the three sorcerers.

"How many times do I have to tell you? I didn't steal the ancient book of spells, I took it to a place of safety. If I hadn't done so, even acting against my own best interests, the situation today would be much worse."

"Perhaps you're speaking the truth. In any case, I'd like to think so, but we'll find out later," concluded Quadehar simply, after a silence. "For the time being, let's concentrate on Robin."

Leaving Qadwan to guard Yorwan, Quadehar and Gerald went over to the group of men assembled around the Commander.

≈ ✳ ≈ ✳ ≈

"Master, what are we going to do?"

"Nothing, for the moment."

The shadowy silhouette gazed down from the top of the Tower at the Knights of the Brotherhood defying him outside the city walls.

"Nothing, Master?" asked Lomgo in surprise. "But . . ."

"I've been expecting it. It was inevitable. . . . Only they've arrived sooner than I anticipated. . . ."

The Shadow's whispering ceased. He was thinking.

"Bring in our friend . . . now. . . ."

Lomgo bowed and set off down the stairs.

After a long moment, puffing and blowing like a whale and cursing the height of the keep, a wild giant of a man appeared on the flat roof. He had a shock of unruly hair, and wore a suit of battered black armor.

"I hope that your men are in position, Thunku. . . ."

"They are, High Priest," thundered Commander Thunku.

"Excellent, excellent. . . . I shall muster mine . . . and we'll wait for the enemy to attack."

"Do you think they've come to attack us?" asked Thunku. He shot a look of scorn in the direction of the knights.

"There are no more than a handful of them!"

"Believe me, Thunku . . . they'll attack. I know them well . . . they'll attack."

The Shadow snickered and Thunku, who was not in the least bit frightened of his master's menacing grin, gave a sinister laugh that could be heard for miles.

Down on the plain, despite the valor in their hearts, the knights were unable to repress a shudder.

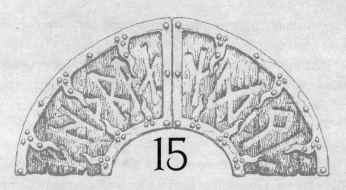

15

URIAN PENMARCH

Yorwan's suggestion that they should negotiate, which Quadehar and Gerald conveyed to the knights' leaders, did not please the straightforward men of action, except perhaps for Valentino, the wisest of them.

"What?" exclaimed Urian. "You want to reason with those madmen?"

"It would give us the opportunity to assess the forces at the city's disposal," argued Quadehar, faced with the elderly knight who looked as if he were about to explode with anger.

"Don't you have faith in the knights' bravery?" the Commander asked the sorcerer in an aggressive tone.

"That's not the issue," said Gerald. "Master Quadehar is not questioning your courage. But according to Yorwan, the priests of Yenibohor have magic powers that . . ."

"Yorwan!" sneered Urian. "Such a cowardly attitude could only come from him! What amazes me, Quadehar, is that you allow yourself to be manipulated by this man when he has already betrayed us in the past."

"That's enough, Urian!" snapped Quadehar. He was losing patience with the giant's attitude. "Your insinuations are unhelpful," he went on.

"Well then, I refuse to obey the Guild and its ridiculous sorcerers!" stormed Urian.

Infuriated, Quadehar took a step toward Urian, a menacing look in his eye. Gerald, the Commander, and Valentino promptly stepped between the two men. And Ambor and Bertolen, the two captains, stood by, uncertain of what to do. Confusion spread among the assembled knights. Here they were, stationed outside the terrible city of Yenibohor, home to all manner of dangers, and their leaders were arguing. This was unsettling to say the least.

"That's enough!" announced Urian.

He extricated himself from the Commander's restraining hold, and retreated a few steps.

"I know what I have to do!"

The giant strode over to a huge rock. He clambered onto it and addressed the astonished knights in thundering tones:

"Knights! My nephew's abductor is hiding in this city! A city occupied by a handful of spineless priests! And what are the sorcerers of the Guild suggesting, on the advice of the traitor Yorwan? That we negotiate!"

A murmur of disapproval rose up from the knights, who were stirred by Urian Penmarch's rallying call to war.

"Aren't you the best fighters of the three Worlds?" he went on, his eyes blazing with excitement and fury. "Aren't you capable of taking this city?"

This time, his words were greeted with an enthusiastic clamor. The men brandished their swords and shields.

"So chaaarge!" cried Urian, raising his axe. "Let's take revenge on those who have dared defy The Lost Isle and the Brotherhood!"

"Attack!"

The coarse cries of the two hundred knights echoed across the plain. Urian placed himself at their head and charged wildly in the direction of the city gates, which stood wide open. The knights rushed after him.

"This is madness," wailed Quadehar, watching the scene, powerless to stop them.

The Commander looked crushed.

"I'm so sorry. There was nothing I could do. Urian is a legendary hero for the knights and they are too impatient for action."

Ambor and Bertolen, fired up like the others by Urian's speech, had been the first to follow his lead.

The Commander turned from his companions and headed toward the city. Valentino followed in his footsteps.

"These are my men," apologized the Commander. "I can't desert them."

"I'll go with you," said Quadehar abruptly. "You'll need me if the priests use magic."

"That's madness, too," protested Gerald, hurrying to catch up.

"I know," admitted the Master Sorcerer sadly. "But I've already abandoned my companions once, at Jaghatel. Today I'll share their fate, whatever that may be. If things go wrong, shelter in the Haunted Forest and then go back to The Lost Isle."

Gerald, Qadwan, and Yorwan watched him enter Yenibohor behind the knights. They were deeply distressed.

"I think we should set out for the Haunted Forest straight away," said Yorwan despondently.

≈ ✳ ≈ ✳ ≈

Urian entered the city followed by the two hundred knights of the Brotherhood of the Wind, with Valentino, Quadehar, and the Commander bringing up the rear. The approach to the massive gate was deserted. They ran another hundred yards or so, then crossed a stone bridge spanning a wide moat. Urian came to a halt in the middle of an avenue and swore. Behind him, the warriors in turquoise armor stopped and began to whisper among themselves. There was nobody about. Silence reigned. The silence of death. It seemed highly likely that this was an ambush.

"What have I done? Confound it, what have I done?" lamented Urian, gradually regaining his senses as the reality of the situation hit him like a cold shower.

"About turn!" he roared to his companions. "Let's get out of this trap, fast!"

But at that moment, the heavy gates shut with a sinister clang that sounded like a death knell. And then dozens of creatures appeared in the surrounding streets, yelling and rushing at the knights. . . .

They were Orks, the terrifying, powerful, humanoid monsters with reptilian faces and hard, scaly skin. Clad in canvas and leather, they wore pendants bearing the symbol of the city of Yadigar, a roaring lion surrounded by flames.

Quadehar, a little behind, recognized the insignia. He turned pale.

"Thunku's men! Again!" he exclaimed.

"We're done for!" muttered the Commander, as the gangs of monsters fanned out along the avenue and occupied the bridge, trapping the knights in a stranglehold.

"We must break free and retreat!" said Valentino, trying to keep calm. "It's our only chance. . . ."

"I'll take care of the gates," announced Quadehar, turning around.

But at that moment a giant Ork barred his path. Instinctively, the sorcerer used the Graphem Thursaz on him. But it had no effect.

"Well I'm stunned!" said Quadehar in amazement. "But I invoked the Uncertain form of the Graphem!"

He tried once again to knock out his opponent with the Graphem, leaping aside to avoid a violent blow from the Ork's sword. To no avail . . .

"Yorwan was right!" he exclaimed. "There's magic at work here that neutralizes my own!"

The sorcerer deflected another blow from the Ork and ran at him. He managed to slit his throat and take his weapon — a heavy sword with teeth like a saw. Then he turned to his companions, who were locked in combat with the monsters. It was a bloody battle.

Another Ork spotted him and rushed at him with a blood-curdling howl, brandishing his nail-studded club. The sorcerer sighed and waited to parry the blow, holding his sword high.

16

ORKS VERSUS KNIGHTS

The Ork rushing headlong toward Quadehar was nearly two heads taller than him. But it took more than that to frighten the Master Sorcerer, who had already fought more than enough grisly creatures in The Uncertain World. He allowed the Ork to advance and leaped nimbly aside at the last minute. As the monster's club hit the ground, he thrust his sword into its stomach. Without so much as a glance at his dying opponent, he swung around to fend off a third Ork. He countered the first blow with his sword, and jumped agilely into the air to avoid the second, then, as he landed, he used his full weight to kick the monster in the knee. The bone snapped sharply with a horrible cracking sound and the Ork rolled on the ground, moaning in pain. Quadehar barely had time to catch his breath before he heard his friends call for his help.

There was fighting everywhere. The knights' reputation remained untarnished even though it was three against one. They fought valiantly and their swords were red with the monsters' blood.

When one of their companions fell, they became even more incensed and fought back all the more furiously. Urian Penmarch, back to back with Valentino, who was covering his rear, was the fiercest: Sword in one hand, axe in the other, his beard thick with dust and frothing at the mouth, he felled the Orks one after the other with the force of a Titan. The Commander also dealt mortal blows to the enemy. His aim was cool, methodical, and precise. The scars streaking his veteran's face gleamed in the sun. Accustomed to being partners, Ambor and Bertolen, back to back like most of the knights, fought like lions. But the battle was lost before it was begun, and they all knew it. There seemed no end to the number of Orks, and each fallen Ork was replaced by another.

"Commander! My magic is powerless!" puffed Quadehar. "We must try to disengage. We can't hold out much longer!"

The sorcerer aimed the point of his sword at a monster's throat. He heard a stifled howl.

"Do you see a place we can retreat to?" asked the Commander, averting an axe blow and smashing the Ork's nose with his elbow.

"I noticed a temple nearby. We could try and shelter there. . . ."

"OK," agreed the Commander, and promptly issued a few curt orders.

Protecting themselves as best they could with their shields, the knights regrouped and slowly began their retreat. The Commander and Quadehar, soon joined by Ambor and Bertolen, led the way. Urian and Valentino brought up the rear. The bloody smell of battle caught in the fighters' throats.

"We're nearly there!" shouted the sorcerer to encourage the men as they turned onto a small side street.

Soon they were able to move faster. The houses protected them from attacks from the sides, and only the rear was vulnerable.

They reached the building spotted by Quadehar, a huge square block in dressed stone, higher than the neighboring houses. It seemed to be some kind of temple or holy place. The door was firmly locked, but a knight soon found a ladder standing against a wall in the courtyard. One after the other, the men in turquoise armor climbed up to the roof and occupied it like a rampart.

"Let's go," Urian said to Valentino. They had stayed until the last, to cover their companions' ascent.

The giant turned around and grabbed the ladder. But he didn't see the Ork that had appeared on the other side of the street and was now making straight for him, brandishing a stake.

"Urian! Watch out!" yelled Valentino, stepping in between his friend and the monster.

The Ork stabbed Valentino brutally in the stomach. The stake pierced his armor and the warrior soundlessly crumpled to the ground.

"Valentino!" howled Urian, leaping down from the ladder. "Valentino!"

He drove back the Ork with a blow from his axe as the beast tried to attack him. Then he picked up his friend. There was a large red stain on the ground. Urian snapped the wooden lance where it had pierced through the armor, slung the unconscious butler over his shoulder, and climbed up onto the roof.

A hundred or so knights had managed to reach the top of the building, and had taken up positions covering the access points to prevent attack. The other fighters had remained on the battlefield, dead, wounded, or taken captive. The Commander took a deep breath. Even though there were heavy losses, it could have been worse.

Quadehar busied himself beside Valentino along with Urian, who was sobbing his heart out, hiccuping like a child.

"I killed him," wept the distraught giant. "I killed them all. . . . It's my fault, it's all my fault. . . . As a result of my pride, my craziness . . ."

"There's no point in feeling sorry for yourself," said Quadehar harshly. "What's done is done, and your irresponsible actions will be judged later. Give me a hand instead."

They undressed the elderly servant, who looked even thinner without his armor. The point of the stake was embedded deep in his stomach.

"He's lost a lot of blood," said Quadehar, deeply concerned. The sorcerer rummaged in the pocket of his cloak and took out a handful of dried herbs, which he moistened with his saliva and applied gently around the wound.

"It's a nasty injury," he confirmed.

"We must save him!" Urian wailed. "We must!"

"If I had an iota of power here," replied Quadehar, attempting to place a comforting hand on the giant's shoulder, "I'd be able to promise you I would. But without Graphems to boost the action of the medicinal plants . . . I very much doubt whether they'll do any good. We must wait, Urian. I can't do any more."

At that very moment, the Orks swarmed up a dozen ladders and onto the rooftop, but the knights drove them back without too much difficulty. A few arrows landed on the roof, fired inaccurately from a neighboring building. The knights sheltered behind their shields and soon the arrows stopped. The hordes of Orks had been forced back, but the knights were under no illusion. . . .

"All they have to do is wait," grumbled Bertolen. "We have no food or water."

But the masters of Yenibohor had other plans. Perched on a rooftop not far from the knights, an imposing man hailed them in a booming voice:

"Any resistance is pointless. You are doomed! I could let time take its toll, but I am impatient by nature."

"It's Commander Thunku, the tyrant of Yadigar," Quadehar informed them. "He's leading the enemy."

The information spread among the knights like wildfire.

"That makes me feel better somehow," admitted Ambor to his friend Bertolen. "I'd have found it disturbing that mere priests were capable of getting the better of the Knights of the Brotherhood. . . ."

"What on earth's going on?" asked Bertolen, as twenty or so men in turquoise armor were brought out to Thunku. They were in chains and flanked by Orks who were armed to the teeth.

Thunku spoke again:

"As you can see, I've taken a few prisoners. I demand that you lay down your arms and surrender. I'm going to count to two hundred. With each ten, I shall kill one of your men until you obey. One . . . two . . ."

"Commander, we must surrender," urged Ambor. "We are done for, in any case. There's no point letting our companions die for nothing!"

"You're right, of course," agreed the Commander. He turned toward Thunku and shouted: "Stop! We surrender."

Thunku was up to nine, and an Ork was already wielding an axe over the head of the knight kneeling before him. The master of Yadigar signaled to the monster to back off, and allowed the prisoner to get to his feet.

"Wise decision, Commander! Leave all your weapons on the roof and come down to the street one by one."

"We've had it. I can't see any way out...," whispered Quadehar in the Commander's ear.

He donned Valentino's armor and disguised his face by smearing it with blood and dust.

In Thunku's eyes he was Azhadar the Demon, and the brute hated him with a vengeance. Better make sure Thunku didn't recognize him.

17

TAKING STOCK

"It's too awful!" wailed Coral, hiding her eyes against Romaric's shoulder as he clumsily tried to comfort her.

"What happened? Is Quadehar . . . ?" Amber hardly dared venture, glancing anxiously at Godfrey.

"What about my uncle Urian?" asked Romaric, his voice trembling.

"We're too far away," replied Godfrey, who had clambered up onto a rock to get a better view. "I can't tell who's survived. . . ."

From the hills where they were hiding, the friends from The Lost Isle hadn't witnessed the battle inside the walls, although the clamor from the city gave them an idea of the fierce fighting going on, but they had seen the roof scene and the Brotherhood's defeat.

"Those weren't priests lying in wait for our friends in that back street, were they?" asked Agatha.

"No," said Godfrey. "Those were Orks. Probably mercenaries brought in as backup by the priests, that's the usual practice in The Uncertain World."

"Who would have imagined that the Brotherhood could lose a battle?" said Thomas pensively.

"The Orks outnumbered them by far," commented Romaric.

"And besides," added Bertram, "maybe the priests intervened with their powers. . . ."

"Orks or priests," fumed Amber, "what does it matter now that the knights are all dead or prisoners?"

"Calm down, Amber," said Bertram. "We're just talking. . . ."

"Yes, and that's all we're doing. That's what's making me so mad!"

"So, what's next?" asked Agatha to stop them from arguing.

"I have no idea," Amber confessed. "I really don't know. . . ."

≈ ✳ ≈ ✳ ≈

"What do we do now?" asked Yorwan.

He and his two companions were hiding behind a rock. They, too, had witnessed the roof scene.

Gerald made no reply. He turned to Qadwan, who shrugged helplessly.

"The only reasonable thing would be to go back to The Lost Isle!"

"And desert Robin?" exclaimed Qadwan.

He shook his head in disbelief.

"It's the only option open to us," said the sorcerer, trying to justify himself as he wiped his glasses. "Once we're back home we'll inform the Provost, who will no doubt call a meeting of the Great Council and . . ."

". . . and a decision will be taken in six months' time! No way. It'll be too late."

"You're right," admitted Gerald. "But the fact is . . . I don't see any solution other than going back to The Lost Isle."

"I do," announced Yorwan.

Lord Sha had thought that nobody would listen to him, but seeing the expectant look on their faces, he realized that the sorcerers were ready to clutch at any straw of hope.

They sat down out of view from the city, and Yorwan began:

"Since my youth, I have belonged to the Bear Society, a very ancient, secret fraternity which exists in all three Worlds. It was founded when the *Book of the Stars* arrived on The Lost Isle. It is thought that the Society was set up by the same people who brought the Book. It then extended to The Real World and The Uncertain World. Its sole aim is to watch over the *Book of the Stars* and the uses to which it is put, for the Book contains spells that could be used for evil. Unimaginable evil. There are not many members of the Society, but we are very influential and we have considerable backing, especially in The Uncertain World, where sinister forces have been plotting against the Book for a very long time. I volunteer to inform the head of the Bear Society and ask for their help. I don't know if that will be enough to fight against the powerful priests of Yenibohor, but . . . there's no harm in trying."

An astonished silence greeted Yorwan's suggestion.

"It's incredible!" exclaimed Qadwan after a while. "I've never heard of this Bear Society, and yet all secrets usually come to the ears of Gifdu!"

"A secret society set up by the same people who brought the *Book of the Stars* . . ." mused Gerald aloud. "Power and an opposition force . . . a remedy, and an antidote for when the remedy turns into poison . . . It makes sense, and what's more, it's very wise!"

"What about you? What's your role in the Bear Society?" Qadwan asked Yorwan, knitting his brow.

"I used to be the Society's secret correspondent in the Guild, on The Lost Isle. Now I'm its eyes and ears in The Real World."

"Was . . . was your disappearance from The Lost Isle with the *Book of the Stars* connected with the Bear Society?" asked Gerald, with a gleam in his eye. The sorcerer was beginning to understand.

"Yes," murmured Yorwan, with a hint of sadness in his voice. He bowed his head. "But I'll tell you about all that later. We're short of time and, since you agree, I'd better contact my friends in The Uncertain World."

≈ ✳ ≈ ✳ ≈

Meanwhile, in the hills, Amber shrieked triumphantly. She'd just had an idea!

"The knights attacked the priests to rescue Robin, and they failed," she declared.

"How can you be so certain that Robin is in Yenibohor?" Agatha butted in.

"Well, if the Brotherhood invaded the city, it's certainly not because it's sales time in the stores!" retorted Amber with a shrug.

"Go on, Amber," encouraged Romaric.

"So the knights' failure forces us to take matters into our own hands," she finished.

"Especially since the fall of the Brotherhood can only mean

one thing. We don't have long to rescue Robin," Godfrey added darkly.

"But how?" puzzled Agatha. "How can we succeed where two hundred knights failed?"

Amber gave her a radiant smile. "We have friends in The Uncertain World, don't we? Godfrey, I'm thinking of Tofann, your giant from the Steppes. Coral, there's Wal and the People of the Sea. And Robin's told us enough about the Men of the Sands and the debt they owe him."

Godfrey's face suddenly lit up.

"You want us to go and find all our friends and ask for their help?"

"Exactly!" said Amber, crossing her arms proudly.

"Yes, but we don't know anybody!" Thomas burst out.

"That's a point," said Bertram.

"Simple," replied Amber, determined to take charge of things. "Seeing as we're short of time, as Godfrey said — and I'm sure he's right — we can't all go together. So let's split into teams. Coral and Romaric, you go and look for your friends among the People of the Sea. Agatha will go with Godfrey in search of Tofann. Thomas, Bertram, and I will head for the Ravenous Desert."

"And what if we don't find anybody?" fretted Coral.

"The Uncertain World isn't that big. Besides, you know where to look. Let's set a date to meet up again, whether we find our friends or not."

Amber's suggestion was put to the vote. It was accepted unanimously. Bertram, who was awake now, said with a mysterious smile:

"I won't be going with you, Amber."

"What?"

"I have another idea. I need to act alone. . . ."

"What on earth are you talking about, Bertram?" pressed Amber.

"Forget it. Just trust me."

They all stared at him anxiously, but were unable to make him change his mind, no matter how hard they tried.

The young sorcerer gathered his belongings and left hurriedly, saying that he mustn't hang around if his plan were to have a chance of succeeding.

≈ ✳ ≈ ✳ ≈

The knights surrendered to Thunku's Orks, who had lain in wait for them at the base of the temple where they had sought refuge. They were manhandled, disarmed, and put in chains, then led down to the city's underground chambers and thrown into damp jails.

"Is everybody all right?" inquired the Commander through the bars on the door of the cell where he had been flung with a dozen of his men.

He received a positive reply from all the cells except the one next to his.

"Valentino is dying," announced Quadehar sadly.

Disguised in the turquoise armor of a knight, the sorcerer had not been spotted, not even when he had walked right under Thunku's nose. Fortunately he had been able to persuade the Orks to allow him to carry the fatally wounded knight on his shoulder, which had helped him conceal his identity . . . even though the shaved-headed priests of Yenibohor in their white robes had looked for the sorcerer among the knights. They thought they had glimpsed him during the battle and had instantly activated their magic powers to neutralize the magic of the stars. Quadehar was glad he'd had the sense to hide his sorcerer's cloak in a crevice on the roof. The priests had finally given up, disappointed.

The Commander took a roll call. Out of the two-hundred-strong force, there were a hundred and twenty-five surviving knights, some forty of whom had minor injuries.

"It's the worst defeat the Brotherhood has ever suffered," the Commander told Ambor, who shared his cell.

"The battle's lost but not the war!" retorted the fiery captain.

"Maybe," said another, dubiously. "But the problem is that we're no longer in a state to carry on the war!"

"What are our chances, Commander?" asked a voice from another cell.

"Slender. I shan't pretend otherwise," was the reply. "But there is some hope. Gerald and Qadwan, the two Master Sorcerers, are free and outside the city. I don't doubt for a moment that they have already come up with a plan. I reckon they'll have gone back to The Lost Isle and will come back with reinforcements."

Despite the uncertainty, the Commander's words comforted the dejected knights.

18

THE BALANCE OF LIGHT

Robin emerged from the faint into which he had lapsed after the frenzied attack by the Shadow spirits. His head throbbed and his throat was burning. He quenched his thirst by drinking copiously.

He felt better. He was surprised and relieved to see that the magic barriers battered by The Shadow had rebuilt themselves. The Armor of Egishjamur, strengthened by Odala, the Graphem that protects enclosed spaces, was giving out its reassuring blue light. The cold red flames of the eight branches of Hagal, the Great Mother, were quietly crackling. And set deep in the stone beneath him he could still feel Mannaz, the link with the Powers, the stellar sphere that had placed him firmly beyond his enemy's grasp.

Amazing. Robin would have expected his magic defense to crumble after The Shadow's onslaught, especially given the weak condition he was in. For it was the Ond, the breath of life, that imparted energy to the Graphems and made the spells effective.

A strong sorcerer made strong magic, and a weak sorcerer, weak magic. It was weird . . . it was as though the Graphems had a life of their own and had renewed the spells without his intervention. It was almost as if the Graphems were protecting him.

Robin didn't waste any effort wondering or seeking explanations: It was fine with him. In his condition, he wouldn't have been able to stand up to another assault by his ruthless enemy without the help of the Graphems.

When The Shadow entered the room again, he was visibly shaken to discover that Robin's magic defenses were as good as new.

"Fine . . . excellent, boy . . . I hope you used up a lot of energy . . . to restore your spells. . . ."

There was now something almost jubilant in The Shadow's whisperings that worried Robin even more than the anger he had shown on the previous visit.

"I feel in good form today. One victory leads to another . . . isn't that so, boy . . . ?"

"What do you mean?" asked Robin weakly, which seemed to delight his opponent.

"I love watching turquoise flowers perish . . . in fields of dust. . . ."

The Shadow's words were even more unfathomable than usual, and Robin decided to let it drop.

"You shouldn't have gone to so much trouble with your walls . . . ," continued The Shadow, changing his tune. "Soon you'll be the one to destroy them . . . and come running to me. . . ."

"Oh really!" cried Robin bravely.

The Shadow snickered. He sat down against a wall of the cell, or at least that was Robin's impression; at that distance, he could barely make him out.

"Let's chat for a while, shall we . . . ? We have so much to talk about. . . ."

The hollow voice had become tender and affectionate. Robin felt uncomfortable.

"Tell me, my boy . . . Talk to me about your parents . . . How are they?"

Robin's heart began to race.

"I have nothing to say to you! My life is none of your business!"

"On the contrary, boy . . . on the contrary. Tell me, is your mother still as pretty as she used to be? The fair Alicia . . . with such soft skin . . ."

Robin opened his mouth in dismay. How did he know? And what did his insinuations mean? "Shut up!" he cried.

The Shadow's voice grew even softer.

"I have every right, my boy . . . especially the right to talk to you about your mother. . . ."

"No! Not about my mother!"

Robin's head was spinning; his thoughts chased each other around and around, colliding, eluding him. He felt as if there was a hand with sharp fingernails inside his chest, clawing at his heart.

"Let's talk about your father, then. . . ."

"My father? Why about my father?"

Robin was close to tears.

"Why . . . ? You ask me why? Come, come, my boy. . . .

Because your father, whom you have never met . . . your father whose identity has always been kept from you . . . the man who loved your mother, Alicia . . . your father, Robin . . . IS ME. . . ."

"NO! NO! NO! NO! NO! NO! NO!"

Robin clutched his head and howled. He was going mad. His father, this monster, this devil? It wasn't possible! He refused to believe it. He shouldn't believe it!

But . . . suppose it was true? If that was the case, why didn't he put an end to all this misery? Why didn't he smash the barriers and rush to him and embrace him?

The Armor of Egishjamur began to glow brightly and Hagal burned more vigorously . . . as if to warn Robin, who had wobbled to his feet.

"Come, my boy . . . come and hug your father. . . . Robin . . . my son . . ."

Robin took one step, and then another, toward The Shadow, as if in a dream. Now everything was clear: His long-lost father was there, on the other side of the walls he had stupidly built! His father was waiting for him, wanted to embrace him. It was all over. . . .

Just then, a Graphem materialized in Robin's mind. A Graphem in the form of scales, with an aura of burning light. Teiwaz, the sign of Irmin, balance, law and order, the invincible principle of world justice and harmony.

As soon as it took shape in Robin's mind, the Graphem destroyed the insidious invisible magic that The Shadow had injected into his words. A terribly gentle spell that stopped Robin from reasoning normally and deprived him of his will, transforming him into a docile puppet.

Teiwaz worked efficiently at restoring calm and reason to Robin's mind.

Soon The Shadow saw Robin hesitate, then retrace his steps.

"What are you waiting for . . . my son?"

There was a note of anxiety in the whispered words. Teiwaz swept away the magic particles that accompanied The Shadow's words before they reached Robin's mind. The apprentice gradually recovered his wits.

If The Shadow were his father, why had he tried to harm Robin by unleashing his magic against him during their previous encounter? A father does not act like that toward his son! His son . . .

Then the truth suddenly dawned on Robin. Alicia wasn't his real mother! He had known it since Lord Sha's revelations and especially since she herself had told him about the stolen baby in the hospital. He knew it, and he had resigned himself to the evidence. Even if the mere idea that this woman, whom he loved more than anyone else in the world, was not his mother, choked him with pain. . . .

He knew it, but The Shadow didn't.

The Shadow had certainly done his homework. He knew Alicia's name and what she looked like. He knew that Robin had never seen his father. He had tried to trick him! And had nearly succeeded. . . . How could he have fallen into such an obvious trap? How could he have been tempted to embrace this monster?

Robin, unaware of how much he owed to Teiwaz's efforts against his tormentor's devious magic, turned toward the spot where he could make out the seated form of The Shadow, his face red with anger:

"I won't come! You are not my father!"

The Shadow knew that Robin had slipped out of his grasp.

Somehow he had lost the boy, just when he had been on the brink of success.

The Shadow howled with rage and started hurling balls of black flame against the Armor.

"Just you wait . . . when I come back, you'll beg me to kill you . . . it'll be less painful. . . ."

The dark form stirred and headed for the door, which opened and closed with a bang. Robin allowed himself a satisfied grin: He had held out against The Shadow for another day.

19

THE SPRING

"So how are we going to find your friends?" asked Romaric, who was, understandably, wondering how on earth they were going to be able to locate a few rafts floating somewhere in the middle of the Infested Sea.

They had set off from the Gray Hills at dawn. Leaving Yenibohor behind them, they were climbing the slope to the northeast.

"I have an idea," said Coral sweetly.

"And what's that?"

"You'll see."

Romaric sighed. He didn't like it when Coral acted all mysterious. What did she imagine? That he was going to beg her to tell him what she was plotting? He went into a silent sulk, but wasn't able to keep it up for long.

"Go on, Coral, tell me! We're partners, aren't we? Yes or no?"

"Ah! Now that's an interesting question!"

Coral stopped and watched him, bowing her head slightly.

She was stunning with her big blue eyes and her windblown long dark hair. Romaric felt awkward.

"What do you mean?" he asked.

"Me? Nothing. What about you? Did you want tell me something?" Coral flashed him a winsome smile.

Romaric melted inside. He had known it wasn't a very good idea to set off alone with this girl who . . . this girl who . . . this girl who he dreamed about all the time. Who with a single look could stop his heart dead, and then set it thumping as if it would burst. Who exasperated him sometimes, but more often made him feel full of joy. Who caused his friends to smile knowingly and tease him, but whom he missed dreadfully when she was far away . . . The fact was, he wouldn't have left her with anyone else for anything in the world. And anyway, what did it matter if he didn't know where they were going? He was with her, and that was good enough for him.

"Y-Yes," stammered Romaric at last, "I want to tell you . . . that . . . well, it's no big deal if I don't know where we're going, as long as you know. Because we're together and . . . that's good."

Coral raised an eyebrow, pretending to think about what he had just said. She decided that it was meant to be a compliment and set off again, muttering about boys' stupidity.

≈ ✳ ≈ ✳ ≈

Qadwan paused for a moment to catch his breath. Since Gerald and Yorwan had left him to try and raise a new army against Yenibohor, the elderly sorcerer had been hobbling toward the Haunted Forest, where they had arranged to meet. His job was to set up camp there and welcome the reinforcements as they arrived.

He sighed. His friends' plan seemed so uncertain.

He desperately wished he were back at his gym in Gifdu. After a brief halt, he continued on his way. The Haunted Forest was still a long hike away for his tired old legs.

≋ ✳ ≋ ✳ ≋

Coral and Romaric kept up a steady pace. In the afternoon, they reached the tip of a headland. They weren't very high up, but it was a sharp drop down to the water and the sheer cliffs looked completely inaccessible. Romaric leaned over the edge and glimpsed a trickle of silvery water emerging from the rock down below and splashing into the sea.

"That's it," he declared. "We can't go any further. Should we turn back?"

"No. We're here. All we have to do now is wait."

"Wait? Are you crazy? What about the Gommons?"

Fierce Gommons lurked on all the coasts of The Uncertain World.

"There aren't any here," said Coral calmly, casting around for a place to settle down.

"How can you be so sure?"

"There are no beaches around here. The Gommons like beaches. . . ."

"OK, you're right," admitted Romaric grudgingly. "But why wait, and who are we waiting for? The People of the Sea? Do you know when they are coming?"

"Not exactly, but the tribes of the People of the Sea need fresh water. And there are only three springs along the coast where they can come and stock up without fear of being attacked by Gommons. I know, because my friend Matsi showed them to me on a sort of map. If we wait here, we're bound to meet them."

Romaric was impressed. "How long do you think we'll have to wait?"

Coral thought.

"There are thirty tribes. Once they've stocked up with fresh water, they can hold out for around three weeks. They never all go to the springs at the same time. Can you imagine the lines, with twenty or so rafts in each tribe? There are three springs, so . . . let's just say, we shouldn't have to wait too long. We simply have to ask whoever comes along first to take us aboard and take us to the Sixth Tribe, which is the one Wal and Matsi belong to."

Romaric was at a loss for words. Why did Coral always prove to be exceptional when there were just the two of them? He would so love to have been able to relish in his pride in front of the others.

Directly above the spring they came across a cleft between two rocks that was big enough to shelter them from the wind and offered a clear view over the sea. They settled down there to wait.

"Can I snuggle up to you? We'll both be more comfortable. . . ." Without waiting for an answer, Coral nestled against Romaric's chest.

He sat there rigid for a moment, then finally put his arms around her. She sighed contentedly.

"Are you OK?" he asked, blowing away the dark hairs tickling his face.

Romaric received a yes in reply that made him tremble from

head to foot. He grew bolder and deposited a furtive kiss that she would never feel on those same hairs that blew back onto his cheek. Then he tightened his arms around her.

As night gathered, the temperature dropped. They unrolled the sleeping bags they had taken from Agatha's parents' house along with supplies of food and slid inside, fully dressed.

"Do you think that the People of the Sea will be able to help Robin?" Romaric asked

"I don't know," admitted Coral. "But they hate the priests of Yenibohor, who in the past used to kidnap their children. I'm sure they'll be delighted to help us."

"They do lead a strange existence, don't they?" went on Romaric, who was in a talkative mood. "Spending their lives on rafts trying to avoid the Stingers in the sea and the Gommons along the coast!"

"You know, there never used to be Gommons in The Uncertain World," replied Coral, biting her lip. "We sent them here when the Brotherhood drove them away from The Lost Isle, at the end of the Middle Ages. . . . Long ago, the People of the Sea lived in villages on the coast, like the fishermen we stayed with on The Middle Island. So they had no choice — it was either live on the sea or die on land."

"That's terrible!" said Romaric, aghast, suddenly becoming serious. "I'm sure that nobody on The Lost Isle knows we're responsible for their predicament."

"At first, I was as shocked as you. But Wal, the Keeper of the Salvaged Objects, and Matsi, his daughter, taught me to see things differently. In fact, fate didn't hound them, it simply presented them with two stark choices. In opting for the harder path, they agreed to see their world with fresh eyes. The Stingers who rule over the Infested Sea were their enemies when they were fishermen . . . now they are their protectors. And the Gommons, in keeping them away from the coast, have saved them from the threat of other humans. Nowadays, they don't need to work, they have no master, they come and go as they please. They are free. You see, they have turned their misfortune into something positive."

Coral's passionate speech left Romaric pensive. His own values were those of The Lost Isle, and he was amazed that Coral was able to show such understanding for people who were so very different.

"Maybe we should take turns to keep watch," suggested Romaric, as Coral prepared to snuggle up to him again. "If your friends come tonight, we might miss them!"

"You're right," she agreed. "You take first turn. . . ."

Romaric clasped his arms around her once more and smiled. This beat sentry duty on the ramparts of Bromotul any day!

20

THE MERCHANTS WAY

Godfrey and Agatha left the Gray Hills at the same time as the others. They set off at once toward the southwest, much to Agatha's surprise, for she had heard that the giant Tofann lived on the steppes of the Uncertain North. Godfrey had explained to her that he had thought long and hard, and that he had come to the following two conclusions: The Tofann he knew was too fond of danger and battles to quietly while away his time in the wilderness, and the Uncertain North was much too far away to make the journey in just six days. So he felt it made a lot more sense for them to head for the road from Virdu to Ferghana and ask any merchants they met if they had come across a mercenary resembling Tofann.

Agatha could not fault Godfrey's plan, and they had walked on until evening, when they reached the Merchants Way.

Actually, it was nothing more than a wide dirt track with stretches that were cobblestoned, a reminder of better days when the road had been maintained. Deep ruts were a sign that it was still in regular use, and there was a good reason: It linked Virdu, the city of the Little Men who mined the precious stones that served as currency in The Uncertain World, and Ferghana, the main trade center. In the past, the road had run further west to Jaghatel, but that stretch was now in a state of neglect, and continued south down to Yadigar, now home to the most evil bandits in the land.

Godfrey and Agatha came to a thicket of stunted trees beside the road and decided to wait there in the hope of meeting some merchants who might know of Tofann's whereabouts. If a gang of robbers appeared, they could simply remain hidden among the trees.

"I'm exhausted!"

"You're not the only one. I thought we'd never reach the road."

"Life's crazy, isn't it?" said Agatha, carefully unrolling her sleeping bag on the ground. "If anybody had told me a week ago that I'd be sleeping by a road swarming with bandits, waiting for a handsome barbarian warrior beside a boy I hardly know, I'd have laughed in their face!"

"That's a little melodramatic," replied Godfrey. "We've known each other for a while, don't forget. We met for the first time in Thunku's palace. . . ."

"I wasn't exactly at my best!" Agatha interrupted him, amused. "I was filthy dirty, in chains . . ."

"Maybe, but for once someone was glad to see us when we weren't expected!"

They burst out laughing.

"The second time was in Dashtikazar, at Samain," Godfrey

went on. "I was dancing with a girl who I had to ditch to chase after you on the moor."

"Are you sorry?"

"Let's say . . . we did have fun and games with the Korrigans!"

"You call that fun? Though when I think about it . . . there were some rather hilarious moments, weren't there? Like when Bertram tried to cast a spell. He was so amazed when he realized it hadn't worked!"

"Yes, and when you gave the king the wrong answer, you were so sure of yourself. You should have seen the look on your face when it dawned on you that you were on the wrong track!"

"Oh, that's not funny!"

But they rolled around laughing all the same. Then the memory of their adventures with Robin reminded them that their friend was a prisoner in Yenibohor. . . .

"I hope Robin's all right," sighed Godfrey. "If he's been kidnapped by The Shadow, he must be having a terrible time. Just thinking about it makes me want to punch someone!"

"You're right. I feel the same way. It's so unfair! Robin's the best. There's nobody more generous, more gifted, more . . ."

"What? Are you in love with him?" taunted Godfrey.

"Me? No! Well, yes . . . a little bit," she finally admitted. "But what girl wouldn't fall for Robin? He's so vulnerable and at the same time so strong, so clumsy, and so talented. . . ."

"That's enough!" Godfrey stopped her, laughing. "His poor ears must be burning!"

"Hey, you're not jealous, are you?" teased Agatha.

"Me? Of course not!"

"Yes, of course, I can see you're not," said Agatha, with a half-smile, crawling into her sleeping bag. "See you in the morning, Godfrey. Sweet dreams!"

"Yeah," he grunted in answer. "And you, keep your head screwed on!"

He too got into his sleeping bag, but was unable to fall asleep, despite the exhaustion of the day. Girls really were unbelievable! You're nice to them, affectionate, and attentive, and that's it — they think you're in love with them. What's more, Agatha wasn't even good-looking. Too tall, too skinny. Mouth too large, eyes too black, hair too dark. OK, she was intelligent and she had a strong character. There was also something magnetic about her and, he had to admit, she did have class. But that was all. Godfrey tried to put her out of his mind. Difficult — she was sleeping beside him, and he could hear her regular breathing a few inches from his ear. A night bird hooted. The wind rustled the leaves in the tree just above them. Godfrey smiled. A tune was beginning to form in his mind. . . .

≋ ✳ ≋ ✳ ≋

They were awakened the next morning by the clatter of a convoy going past on the road. They leaped out of their sleeping bags and raced over to the leading cart. A Hybrid mercenary, a cross between an Ork and a human, growled in surprise and raised his sword. He lowered it the minute he saw they were children and gave them a disdainful look. The driver, a jovial-looking man, stopped his vehicle by yanking the reins and making soothing noises to the two huge golden oxen that were pulling it.

Godfrey spoke to him in Ska, the language of The Uncertain

World. He asked if by any chance he knew a warrior answering to the name of Tofann who used to work as a mercenary for the merchants of Ferghana.

"A giant from the steppes of the North?" replied the man, scratching his head. "With dragons tattooed on his skull? I know one who set up an escort force to operate along this road a few months ago. He has around twenty men, warriors from the steppes, like himself. They're the best there is. If I'd been able to afford it, I'd have used their services rather than these Hybrids who can only think of getting drunk at each halt!"

"And where can I find this company?" enquired Godfrey, delighted that his hunch had been right.

"On the road, of course! Where exactly, I don't know, but if you're not in too much of a hurry, I suggest you wait. He's bound to come past sooner or later. . . ."

Godfrey and Agatha thanked the man warmly for his information. They made him promise to tell Tofann, if he met him, that a boy called Godfrey was looking for him and was waiting for him in a thicket by the roadside. Then they went back to the shelter of the trees.

"The merchant's right," said Agatha. "We have no idea where your friend is. If we go looking for him, we might go the wrong way and miss him. . . . The best thing is to stay put, and be patient."

Godfrey could see that this made sense. They could wait: They had five days, less one for the return journey. The hardest thing was going to be killing time. If only he'd brought his zither with him!

21

THE RAVENOUS DESERT

On the first day, Amber and Thomas had set off due south. They'd come to the Merchants Way, but had decided not to follow it because it went too close to Yenibohor for their liking. So they'd turned off toward the southeast so as to avoid the evil city as they made their way to the Ravenous Desert. They had spent their first night in an old shepherd's hut in a fallow field.

On the second day, they had crossed the Foaming River and, further on, the Melancholy Water, then tramped through the high grasses of the endless prairie of the Two-headed Sphinx. The two river crossings had cost them many precious stones. First they'd had to pay the ferryman they eventually found after scouring the river banks, and then a man who was fishing from his boat moored on the river bank. Amber and Thomas had no idea where they'd slept on the second night: They had collapsed with exhaustion by a bush with purple berries.

On the third day, they were at last able to make out the glistening yellow sands of the vast desert in the distance.

"Whew! I must say I'm glad we're here at last . . . ," declared Thomas, wriggling his hips to shift the weight of his backpack.

"I'm wiped out, too," replied Amber, glancing at her compass, which had guided them across the wild and rugged terrain. "We made it in fantastic time. But we had no choice. Six days isn't long."

Neither of them was naturally talkative. They had exchanged few words on their journey. They had contented themselves with looks, and, as time went on, smiles.

When Bertram had set off for his mystery destination, Amber had been uneasy about finding herself alone with Thomas, who she thought was a rather clumsy oaf. But very soon a bond developed between them as they tackled the difficulties of the journey together. Amber realized that Thomas had a strong, easy-going personality, and that his gruff, awkward manner concealed a pleasant open-ness and huge generosity. She also became aware that he wasn't able to cope on his own. Thomas needed someone — someone to follow, someone to look up to and worship. First Agatha, then Robin, and now her. Amber felt as if she had been given a new responsibility.

"Lucky we didn't bump into the Two-headed Sphinx!" exclaimed Thomas, shaking his auburn mop of hair.

With their goal in sight, he felt the need to talk. It was his way of showing his relief.

"Don't be stupid, the Sphinx died centuries ago," said Amber. "Killed by farmers who were tired of having their children gob-bled up while they watched over the sheep on the prairie. Robin told me all about it."

"Did that Sphinx also ask riddles? Two, maybe, seeing as it had two heads!"

"I don't know. You'll have to ask the people it ate!"

Amber suddenly went quiet. She had inadvertently uttered Robin's name and that was enough to make her gloomy. They went on in silence.

"Do you miss him badly?" asked Thomas, who had caught the miserable expression on his new friend's face.

"Who?"

"Robin, of course!"

"Of course I miss him," confided Amber, after a moment's hesitation. "So much that I find it hard to explain, even to myself. You see, when he's not with me, I feel as though nothing is of any interest, nothing matters. It's horrible. . . . Do you think he feels that, too?"

"Oh, I'm sure he does."

"Really? How could you know? Has he told you?"

"He hasn't said anything, but there are things that girls see and boys don't, and others that boys see and girls don't. I am a boy, and I can tell you that I've seen how Robin looks at you," said Thomas awkwardly, trying to comfort her.

"It's sweet of you to tell me that, Thomas," murmured Amber, touched. Then she went very quiet, lost in her own thoughts.

A little later they reached the edge of the Ravenous Desert. The prairie stopped dead, like land meeting the sea. There was sand as far as the eye could see, shimmering sand which seemed to be waiting. . . .

"Brrr!" shivered Amber. "To think, this desert will swallow you whole and gobble you up the moment you set foot in it!"

"What are we going to do?"

"Robin told me that the Men of the Sands send each other smoke signals."

"Like the Native Americans in The Real World?"

"Yes."

"And do you know the signals used by the Men of the Sands?"

"No. But I think if we just light a fire, that'll arouse their curiosity and bring them this way."

They began to hunt around for firewood but found none and had to make do with piling up heaps of dry grasses.

"It's even better than wood," declared Amber with satisfaction, as she struck a match and set light to the first heap. "Grass makes more smoke."

It was true; the grass burned instantly, giving off a thick smoke that forced them to step away.

"I hope it's the Men of the Sands who come and not Orks or bandits!" said Thomas.

"The Men of the Sands are the only ones who are able to walk across the Ravenous Desert because they have special stone shoes," Amber reassured him. "And anyway, if some Orks show up, you'll give them a hard time, right?"

Amber's allusion to his act of bravery in Penmarch Forest made Thomas smile.

"I don't know, but one thing's certain, and that is that I'll defend our lives to the death!"

"I don't doubt it for a moment, Thomas. . . ."

They fell silent and concentrated on keeping the fire going.

Please, please come, willed Amber silently, in the direction of the Ravenous Desert. *Robin needs you and we have so little time.*

22

THE TORTOISE WORLD

Curiously, it seemed to Robin that as the hours and maybe even the days went by, he was losing all notion of time. He was not as tired as at the beginning of his captivity, even though he still hadn't eaten and the pitcher of water was almost empty.

Actually, he hadn't had anything to drink for a long time. He wasn't thirsty. A feeling of well-being had come over him when Kenaz, the Graphem of warming fire, Ingwaz the Wealthy, which helped concentrate energy, and Laukaz, the vital fluid, had glowed inside him. Now Robin was convinced: The benevolent Graphems had taken him under their wing and were acting independently.

Once, when he and Master Quadehar had been talking about Charfalaq, the Chief Sorcerer, the Master Sorcerer had told him that there came a point when the body no longer nourished the magic, but the magic nourished the body. This was what seemed to be happening to him

≈ ✳ ≈ ✳ ≈

For the fourth time, The Shadow paused on the threshold of the dark cell.

"Impressive . . . very impressive . . . you should be writhing with hunger and thirst, crawling on the ground, and begging me to put an end to your misery. . . . Instead, I find you alert, calm, and sure of yourself."

Robin made no reply. He was out of reach, protected by the Armor of Egishjamur and Odala, reassured by Hagal's crackling and the presence beneath him of the cosmic sphere of Mannaz. Teiwaz stopped any evil spells from attacking his mind, and Ingwaz, Kenaz, and Laukaz were keeping him alive. The Shadow couldn't get to him. And he knew it!

"To tell you the truth, boy . . . you both infuriate and delight me. I have only one wish, and that is to destroy you, but I can't help admiring you. You force me to test myself to the limit, and I love you for that. Yes, I love you. . . ."

The Shadow started pacing up and down beside the wall of energy.

"I sought the means of defeating you in my books of spells, and I've found the solution. A solution as old as the world . . . as old as this world, anyway. . . ."

Robin was struck by a strange object lying close to the Armor of Egishjamur. He peered through the dark to try and see it more clearly. Actually, there were three objects that The Shadow had placed on the floor: a wooden eagle about six inches high with its wings raised above its head and a menacing hooked beak, a tormented-looking terra-cotta tortoise, and a stone disc covered in signs that were impossible to make out. Robin was puzzled. What did all this mean?

"I'm going to leave you with a new friend. . . . I'd like to have stayed, but I'm afraid it might also attack me."

The Shadow gave an eerie laugh and headed for the door. As he left the room, he rasped out a string of incomprehensible words in a macabre voice. Instinctively, Robin turned to the objects.

The disc was the diameter of a small plate and the thickness of a cookie. It began to wobble. Robin screwed up his eyes. No, he was wrong, it wasn't the disc that was moving, but the signs engraved on it. To his amazement, the signs dropped onto the floor and started marching toward the Armor in a column, like ants. When they came up against the magic wall, the ant-signs clustered together and started gnawing at it. Robin couldn't believe his eyes. A hole soon appeared in the base of the Armor, and then the wooden eagle came to life.

The bird let out a shrill cry as it spread its wings, as if it had been frozen for an eternity. It strutted over to the hole made in the Armor by the ant-signs and pushed its way inside. The Graphem Hagal began to glow red as it had done when The Shadow had destroyed the first barrier so as to place Robin out of danger behind a second wall of energy. The wooden eagle then took wing and perched on top of it. The sinister bird gave another shriek and began to hammer against the magic barrier with its powerful beak. Robin shuddered and huddled in a corner, hugging his knees. He watched the magic wall crack and shatter like a window pane, with a sound of breaking glass. Then the tortoise stirred.

It was about the size of a little pet tortoise and moved with the same lethargy. It turned its head and blinked. Then it opened its mouth and Robin thought he was going mad: The tortoise began to moan!

"Ahhhhhh . . . I'm in pain, such pain! Thank you for waking me up . . . to share my pain!"

The terra-cotta tortoise gazed at Robin with eyes that seemed infinitely ancient, and Robin knew at once that he was powerless, absolutely powerless, against this creature. His heart was filled with bleak despair.

The horrid beast pushed its way through the hole beneath the Armor of Egishjamur and slowly plodded toward him. At once Mannaz encased Robin in the protective sphere and placed him under the protection of the Powers. The tortoise stopped in its tracks. Robin desperately entreated the five elements not to let the creature chew its way through the Graphems' protection.

"I'm in pain, Robin, such pain . . . and you are so good, so good to have awakened me from my sleep . . . to share a little of my burden!"

Robin was panic-stricken. He looked at the tortoise and he understood. He understood that the creature was as old as this world because he was this world — or at least its soul. And he bore all the atrocities, all the pain. And what he intended to do was to pass some of his suffering on to Robin. But Robin's mind wouldn't be able to cope: He would go insane. He howled.

"You're right to be afraid . . . but fear is nothing compared to some things. You'll soon have the time to find out, plenty of time!"

The terra-cotta tortoise did not try to break through the stellar sphere but merely closed its eyes. Robin felt something trying to worm its way inside his head. Teiwaz attempted to resist the intrusion but was soon forced to retreat. It wasn't powerful enough.

Then, from the innermost depths of Robin's being, two other Graphems came to the rescue.

The first was Ansuz, Repulsion and Humidity, which frees from the fear of death and unlocks the ultimate inner resources. The second was Ehwo, the Horse and the Twins, the spiritual vehicle.

Ansuz began by driving the fear from Robin's belly and heart. Then, under the Graphem's gentle but firm influence, Robin fell into the state of ecstasy which the sorcerers called Odhr, which nobody had experienced in living memory.

Finally, while the now enraged tortoise continued its onslaught, Ehwo gently seized Robin's mind and buried it in the regions of the soul to which not even the Powers have access, so as to protect the Odhr into which he had withdrawn.

The tortoise's moans intensified. It turned its anguished gaze on Robin, who was sitting cross-legged, his eyes wide open and gazing at the ceiling.

"He's gone. . . . You have gone, boy. Even if you appear to be here."

With slow, deliberate steps, the terra-cotta reptile turned around, followed by the wooden eagle and the ant-signs, which climbed back onto the stone disc where they arranged themselves in the form of a spiral.

They froze in their original positions, the eagle with its head buried under its wing and the tortoise with its head withdrawn into its shell.

Inside the sphere of Mannaz, behind the shattered walls of Egishjamur and Hagal, Robin sat as motionless as if he, too, were stone.

23

AROUND THE CAMPFIRE

Tofann was in heaven. Godfrey played like a master! And the joyful tunes he coaxed out of a zither transported the giant to The Lost Isle, a place he had never seen but which the music made real. Meanwhile, smiling happily, his scarred and tattooed men clapped their huge hands in time to Godfrey's playing and there was a really festive mood.

Godfrey and his friend Tofann had met up on the Merchants Way, on the morning of the third day.

Until then, Godfrey and Agatha had passed the time chatting and playing chess on an improvised chessboard while they kept an eye on the trade caravans trundling past.

As the merchant had predicted, Godfrey eventually spotted the familiar figure of the Warrior of the Steppes at the head of a magnificent convoy of wagons slowly wending its way along the road. With a yell, he'd rushed to meet him, waving excitedly, much to the amazement of Tofann, who could hardly believe his eyes, and to the disappointment of Agatha, who was beginning to enjoy this time alone with Godfrey.

The giant had given Godfrey a delighted bear hug, almost suffocating him. The twenty warriors of the North guarding the convoy gathered around their chief and gave Godfrey great friendly thumps on the back.

Agatha shyly went over to join them, intimidated by the fierce-looking warriors dressed in leather and metal who sported outrageous tattoos and carried giant swords on their backs. She was particularly nervous of the enormous Tofann with his booming voice, gray eyes, scarred face, and skull tattooed with dragons, but Agatha soon found her customary assurance and spirit and was quickly accepted amid laughter and friendly banter.

"I'll help you," Tofann had promised after Godfrey had told him what he was doing in The Uncertain World. "So will my companions, I'm sure, but I'll have to let them make up their own minds. They are free men who volunteered to join my guard unit. They're not servants. But first of all, we must accompany these merchants who have paid us to escort them safely to their destination. Wait for me here in the woods. I'll come and fetch you when we've finished."

Tofann had kept his word and he and all his warriors turned up the following evening and continued the journey with their friends from The Lost Isle.

So Godfrey and Agatha were the first to arrive at the appointed meeting place in the Gray Hills.

"Ah, musician," sighed Tofann, as Godfrey sang the closing notes of a ballad. "I've missed your skills! I've never come across anyone as gifted as you in this World!"

"You see, Godfrey, you've got a great career ahead of you!" teased Agatha.

"You may laugh," replied Godfrey. "Just you wait, you'll see." He turned to the warriors and spoke to them in Ska, "And now sweet Agatha is going to sing you a song!"

"Are you crazy?" protested Agatha. "No way! I can't . . ."

"You'd better get on with it," cut in Godfrey. "The people of the steppes don't like to be kept waiting. And by the way, they're music lovers. They'll give you a hard time if you sing off-key."

Agatha stared hard at him but couldn't work out whether he was joking or not. Unsure, she rose to the challenge, as she always did.

She asked Godfrey to accompany her on the zither, cleared her throat, then launched into a haunting song that was a favorite on The Lost Isle, about a mother and daughter who go to the forest.

"The daughter sighs, What ails you, Marguerite? I am a girl by day and a white doe by night."

Agatha sang in a low, melodious voice that was deeply moving, and Godfrey was pleasantly surprised. When she finished, the men of the steppes applauded warmly.

They weren't the only ones:

"Well done, Agatha!"

"Yes, that was great!"

They all turned around in unison to see who was lurking in the shadows.

"Romaric! Coral!"

The zither forgotten, Godfrey raced over to greet his friends.

≈ ✳ ≈ ✳ ≈

Romaric and Coral had waited for ages in the shelter of the rocks above the spring, hoping that one of the Tribes of the People of the Sea would come in search of fresh water. After two days, they spotted the rafts of the Fourth Tribe heading for the cliffs. Coral and Romaric had been so deep in conversation and the People of the Sea had been so swift and silent that they had almost finished fetching the water when the pair eventually spotted them. Luckily a child's cry attracted their attention and brought them running from their shelter to see the huge rafts.

Cupping her hands, Coral had called to the men and women, who gaped in astonishment at their sudden appearance on the clifftop above their heads. Luckily, all the Tribes had heard the story of Coral's stay with Wal and Matsi, and the expressions of alarm and fear soon turned into friendly smiles.

The People of the Sea wore few clothes on their tanned bodies and their hair was bleached white by the sun and saltwater. The white membrane covering their eyes that enabled them to see underwater gave them a glassy stare.

The guide, who navigated the Tribe's rafts across the Infested Sea, avoiding strong currents and Stinger jellyfish, told Coral that the Sixth Tribe was a long way off. Coral explained that she and Romaric had to get a message to Wal urgently and the quickest way to do this would be for the Fourth Tribe to take it for them. The guide replied that as soon as his people had filled their water tanks, they would set off to deliver Coral's message. Coral then explained why she was looking for Wal, and Romaric added that if the Sixth Tribe agreed to come and help them, their rafts would be able to sail up one of the creeks at the foot of the Gray Hills, directly to the spot where the friends had all agreed to meet up. The guide promised that they would do their utmost to deliver Coral's message. Romaric and Coral had sensed that the People of the Sea were troubled by their revelations about Yenibohor, the priests, and Robin. Then, seeing that there was nothing more to be gained by hanging around, Coral and Romaric set off for the Gray Hills at a gentle pace.

≈ ✳ ≈ ✳ ≈

"Two whole days to get here from your spring," Godfrey said to Romaric, with a wink. "You must have been very tired!"

"You're right, we didn't hurry," he replied with an embarrassed smile. "But we walked very fast on the way to the spring, and Coral thought we should save our strength for the return, given what's in store. . . ."

"You don't have to make excuses, Romaric," said Coral, giving Godfrey a withering look. "Perhaps Godfrey would like to explain the goofy smile he had on his face while Agatha was singing!"

"Oh-ho!" cut in Tofann, laughing. "By the spirits of the steppe, stop bickering, all of you!"

Godfrey flashed his friend a grateful smile and Coral affectionately slipped her hand into the giant's. They joined the others around the fire. The introductions were made, stories of their travels exchanged and the festive atmosphere was restored. Tofann took out a skin drum from his bag, and the warriors sang a wild song celebrating the rugged beauty of their native steppes.

24

THE GRAY HILLS

In the grove in the Haunted Forest, Qadwan was still keeping watch by the glowing embers of the fire. The sun was slowly rising, trying to break through the tattered mist clinging to the trees.

At last Yorwan and Gerald appeared, accompanied by a stranger dressed in a bearskin.

The elderly sorcerer, pleased to be able to stretch his stiff legs, gave Gerald a hug, shook Yorwan's hand warmly, and made a welcoming gesture toward the newcomer who had remained in the background.

"We've done well," declared Gerald, sounding pleased with himself. "The chief of the Bear Society has agreed to help us."

Intrigued, Qadwan turned to gaze at the mysterious figure. "Let's sit by the fire," he suggested, addressing the stranger directly. "There's still a nip in the air and it'll keep us warm while we talk and get acquainted."

"Excellent idea," agreed their mystery guest, in a voice that was both gentle and firm.

He drew nearer and removed the bear's head covering his face to reveal not a man, but a woman — with long hair and a beautiful face with luminous green eyes.

"Allow me to introduce Kushumai the Huntress, chief of the Bear Society and the resistance against Yenibohor," said Gerald to the dumbfounded Qadwan.

By now it was light, but there was still a chill in the air. Yorwan, draped in his voluminous red cloak, seemed anxious.

"Is something the matter?" asked Gerald.

"I can feel a presence."

"A presence . . . ? What sort of presence?" Gerald continued. "Priests, Orks? The Shadow?"

"No, no, nothing like that," Yorwan reassured him.

"Could it be the reinforcements we're expecting?" asked Kushumai, coming closer.

"No. That's what intrigues me. I've just woven an investigation spell to locate the members of the Bear Society. They should have arrived by now. As for backup forces, the spell has identified a strangely assorted group very close to here."

"Can you pinpoint them?"

"Yes, they're in the hills to the east of the Haunted Forest."

"Right, let's go there," said the Huntress decisively, adjusting her sword at her waist. "If they're a threat, we need to be certain and, besides, being on the move will keep us warm while we wait for our troops to arrive."

≋ ✳ ≋ ✳ ≋

"Well, Romaric? Can you see anything?"

"Not a thing! Normally you can see for miles around from

these hills. If Bertram or Amber were to appear, I'd spot them right away."

"I hope nothing's happened to them," fretted Coral.

"Come on," said Romaric softly, giving Coral a hug. "We've had so many amazing escapes before. There's no reason why it should be any different this time. . . . You'll see, your sister will be here soon and so will that idiot Bertram!"

Coral gave a wan smile and rested her head on Romaric's shoulder. Godfrey came over to them.

"Sorry to spoil such a romantic moment, but Tofann tells me there are some people approaching our camp."

He asked them to follow him, gesturing to them to hurry up. They joined Agatha, who was lying on her stomach amid the Warriors of the Steppes, watching the progress of four figures in the hills. One of them was a woman in a bearskin, another was clad in a strange red cloak, and the other two wore the robes of sorcerers of The Lost Isle.

"Gerald! It's Gerald!" exclaimed Coral excitedly.

"Everything's OK, Tofann," Godfrey said to the giant who was looking at him enquiringly. "They're on our side!"

Then he and his friends stood up and waved madly at the little group ascending the hill.

Gerald thought he was seeing a mirage, even though it wasn't hot and they weren't in the desert! But what other explanation was there for the fact that he thought he could see Godfrey, Romaric, and Coral waving from the hilltop when he had left them on The Lost Isle in Bertram's care? And besides, if they were real, who were those fierce-looking fellows with them?

"Yoo-hoo! Gerald! It's us! We're here!"

No, it wasn't a mirage. The sorcerer couldn't believe his eyes.

While Kushumai seemed delighted at the arrival of this unexpected support in the shape of Tofann and his men, Gerald didn't look exactly thrilled to see the children. Especially when the sorcerer found out that Bertram, Amber, and another boy, Thomas, had also gone off looking for their friends in The Uncertain World and had not been seen since.

Purple with anger, Gerald told them that from now on they'd better do as they were told, without question. Then he walked off with Yorwan, shaking his head.

"I suppose we're lucky he didn't send us back to The Lost Isle," grumbled Agatha.

"We might have been better off," replied Romaric. "Now we've got to behave like good boys and girls and do what the grown-ups tell us!"

"Huh! Not a word of thanks, no recognition for our efforts!" said Coral huffily. "Even though we've brought Gerald all the warriors of the North! And the People of the Sea and the Men of the Sands will be here soon, and . . ."

"Be patient!" broke in Romaric. "The first chance we get, we'll take things into our own hands again!"

"I quite agree," said Godfrey, as annoyed as the others. "But will that chance come?"

"If it doesn't, we'll create it!"

≋ ✳ ≋ ✳ ≋

While Gerald was giving the friends a severe scolding in the Gray Hills, Urian Penmarch was sobbing his heart out inside Yenibohor.

"What's wrong?" asked the Commander.

"It's Valentino," said Quadehar flatly. "He's dead. I'm so sorry, there was nothing I could do. My magic still won't work here."

A painful silence ensued, broken only by Urian's sobs. From one end of the prison wing to the other, a song rose up from a hundred and twenty throats. It was a lament paying tribute to a comrade fallen in battle, a comrade who would never be forgotten by his companions.

Urian crumpled over the lifeless body of the man who had been his brother in arms. Respecting his grief, the other knights in the cell kept their distance. Quadehar let his head loll back against the damp stone wall and sighed. What madness! What chaos . . . Worse than the defeat was the terribly humiliating feeling of being overtaken by events. The sorcerer's heart swelled with anger. How long had the situation been beyond his control? Since the attack at Jaghatel, when he had seen his sorcerer friends die one after the other? Maybe even before that. In truth, since the revelation of Robin's magic powers . . . A number of things Quadehar had believed to be solid had since collapsed, like an object you think you're holding firmly in your hand suddenly crumbling to dust. The invincible Brotherhood had just suffered a crushing defeat, the Guild was corrupted by The Shadow, Valentino was dead and he hadn't been able to prevent it. And Robin? At the thought that somebody might be harming him at that very moment, Quadehar felt a surge of hatred. Amid all the uncertainties plaguing him, his profound affection for the boy was a certainty. . . . He would rescue him. Even if he had to go to Hell itself and defy Bohor in person, he promised he would, and so felt a little calmer.

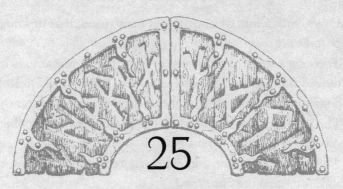

25

ANXIETIES

Kushumai made the decision to set up the base camp for the counterattack in the Gray Hills, which were better situated and easier to defend than the Haunted Forest.

The Huntress had automatically taken charge of operations, much to the relief of Gerald, who was not comfortable in the role of chief. The minute they learned who she was, the Warriors of the Steppes had shown her immediate respect tinged with fear. Despite their resentment toward the ungrateful adults, Romaric, Godfrey, Coral, and Agatha had stared at the young woman clad in a bearskin, first with curiosity and then with admiration when Qadwan told them her identity.

"This woman is the chief of the Bear Society, a secret organization to which Lord Sha also belongs," the elderly sorcerer had told them. "The Bear Society's mission is to protect the three Worlds and prevent the *Book of the Stars* from being used for evil purposes."

Of course Agatha and Coral had immediately pointed out to

the boys, with a hint of smugness in their voices, that this hugely important organization was run by a woman.

Their curiosity had then been aroused by the mysterious man in the red cloak, Lord Sha, also known as Yorwan, whom Robin had mentioned briefly. But he merely smiled at them distantly.

The fact was that Yorwan was busy planning the storming of Yenibohor. He explained his plan of attack to Kushumai.

"Why don't we wait and see what reinforcements my men bring?" objected the Huntress.

"You also sound worried," commented Yorwan. "Do you think there won't be enough of us to take this cursed city?"

"Lord Sha, you know that the Bear Society has always dreamed of putting an end to the plotting and scheming of the people of Yenibohor," replied Kushumai, wrinkling her forehead. "Well, why do you think we haven't done so? Because they are powerful, very powerful. Their wealth has always enabled them to hire the services of the unscrupulous Thunku and his Orks. And then there are the priests, and their mysterious and terrifying High Priest."

"But we are not exactly without resources ourselves," said Yorwan. "We have the support of the entire Uncertain World, which has had enough of the priests' reign of terror. We'll have a large army, there's no doubt about that."

"Maybe," admitted Kushumai. "But is it equal to the task? Don't forget that the two hundred knights from The Lost Isle weren't able to hold out for long against Thunku's Orks, and they are among the best fighters of the three Worlds!"

"The knights ran headlong into an ambush because they hadn't stopped to think about a battle plan," sighed the red-cloaked sorcerer. "This time, it'll be different."

"OK, supposing we managed to overcome the mercenaries in the city, how would we fight the power of the priests? There's only you, Gerald, and me, and perhaps old Qadwan if he's feeling better by then, to combat them. I'm not doubting the strength of your magic, Lord Sha, nor that of Gerald, but even combined, our powers won't add up to much compared with those of the priests."

"So that's what's worrying you," said Yorwan, suddenly understanding. "The limitations of our magic powers . . ."

The chief of the Bear Society contented herself with a nod.

They set up their permanent camp in a sheltered valley close to a hill that gave them a view over the plain, the sea, and the city of Yenibohor in the distance. Silent as jungle cats, the Warriors of the Steppes dispersed to guard the camp with quiet efficiency.

The four friends left Kushumai and the three sorcerers discussing their chances of success, and sat down a little farther away.

"I wonder what my sister can be up to. Why isn't she back yet?" asked Coral anxiously.

"It's a long way to the Ravenous Desert," ventured Romaric, trying to reassure her once more. "Give her time to get back!"

"Romaric's right," said Godfrey. "Bertram's the one we should be worrying about. Did any of you get an idea where he was off to?"

"No, and I'm worried, too," confessed Agatha. "Bertram had that daft smile that usually spells disaster."

"We should never have let him go," said Coral.

"Nonsense . . . trust him," suggested Romaric. "He's already shown us what he's capable of, the best as well as the worst."

"Let's hope that this time it'll be the best!" exclaimed Godfrey with a sigh.

A cloud of dust on the plain signaled the arrival of a large army. Everyone was on the alert.

"They're coming from the west," said Gerald, shading his eyes from the blinding sun with his hands.

"No, from the south," Qadwan corrected him.

In actual fact, two armies were marching toward the Gray Hills.

"Are those the men of Yenibohor?" asked a worried Gerald.

"Yenibohor is to the east," replied Kushumai. "No, I think these are the forces raised by the Bear Society. Lord Sha informed them of the changed meeting place by telepathy."

And indeed, the approaching troops were a mixed bunch, resembling neither Orks nor priests but men of arms, bearing swords, lances, bows, axes, scythes, and sticks.

"How many are they?" asked Qadwan in amazement.

"Hard to say . . . maybe a thousand," replied Yorwan.

Kushumai went to meet the first contingents of armed men to arrive on the scene. They greeted her respectfully.

"Look . . . ," exclaimed Godfrey, spotting a face in the crowd. "I know that tall fair-haired man amid all those redheads. He's the instrument-maker from a village in the West who sold me a zither on our last visit!"

Godfrey went up to the man, who didn't recognize him at first. But when he introduced himself, the man shook his hand warmly.

"So you're a member of the Bear Society?" Godfrey asked him.

"Don't forget what I said one day in my shop to a boy disguised as a Little Man of Virdu — everyone's entitled to have their secrets!"

They laughed at the memory of their first meeting.

There were other surprises in store for the friends from The Lost Isle: courageous farmers from the West and men in armor wearing helmets crowned with animal skulls, said to be Kushumai's bodyguards, as well as a hundred or so bandits with rugged, scarred faces who went around shaking hands with their unlikely new allies. Godfrey recognized the archer, the young bandit who had confronted Tofann when he and his fellow brigands had ambushed them on the road to Yadigar. The giant had spared his plucky opponent, merely wounding him. Tofann and the archer seemed pleased to see each other, the giant recalling the bandit's bravery, and the archer, the warrior's generosity in allowing him to escape with his life.

Next to the archer stood a boy who was staring at them round-eyed, as if the sky had just fallen on his head.

"Toti!" screeched Coral, recognizing the young page who had been held prisoner at the same time as them in Thunku's jail in Yadigar.

They rushed over to their friend in utter disbelief and dragged him to one side. While the rest of the Bear Society poured into the camp in the hills, they told each other about their adventures. They discovered that Toti was the archer's brother and that both of them were informers for the Bear Society, one among the bandits and the other inside Thunku's palace. Toti shuddered and applauded when they told him of Robin's exploits in Commander Thunku's palace. Nobody in The Uncertain World had ever understood why it had collapsed. He was over the moon to be reunited with his friends. Only the absence of Robin and Amber cast a shadow over the occasion.

"Oh! If you knew how happy I am! I was really afraid of finding myself all alone surrounded by brutes and soldiers, like last time in the palace prison!"

"Don't worry, we're here and we're all together," replied Romaric comfortingly. "And I promise you we won't be bored, just as we weren't bored in Yadigar!"

As dusk fell, a thousand men determined to vanquish Yenibohor's armies set up camp in the Gray Hills. The only people missing were Bertram, Amber, and Thomas.

26
COUNCIL OF WAR

"Coral! Hey, Coral . . ."

Qadwan gently shook Coral, who was asleep beside her friends, curled up in her sleeping bag. The little group had wisely withdrawn to a quieter spot when the campfires had been lit and the men had begun to laugh, sing, and argue.

"What is it?" she groaned, trying to open her eyes.

"Someone's looking for you, someone who's desperate to see you."

It took Coral a moment to wake up properly. Dawn was just breaking through the cloudy sky. Blinking, her hair tousled, she hastily pulled on her clothes, got up, and with an envious glance at her sleeping companions, followed the elderly sorcerer.

Qadwan led her to the crest of the hill where Kushumai had set up her command post. At her side stood Gerald wearing the dark cloak of the Guild, Yorwan swathed in the red mantle of Lord Sha, Tofann clad in leather and metal, the Hunter of the Purple Forest in light armor, the instrument-maker wearing the thick canvas of the farmers of the West, and the archer in a motley get-up made of various items stolen from the victims of his robberies. All seven stood facing a tiny figure who did not seem in the least intimidated and who rushed up to Coral and gave her a hug the minute she saw her.

"Coral! Coral!"

"Matsi? But . . . but . . . ," stammered Coral, hugging the little girl with white hair and eyes.

"The people of the Fourth Tribe gave us your message," explained Matsi, delightedly stroking the face of the only true friend she had ever had.

"You mean your Tribe has come to help us? Oh, that's wonderful!"

"Not my Tribe, no," Matsi corrected her. "My father managed to assemble all thirty Tribes for an extraordinary general meeting. You know, we don't like the priests of Yenibohor at all. For many years they used to kidnap the children of the People of the Sea when we landed on their coast. . . ."

"I know, your father told me. And then . . . ?"

"Then my people decided to send our hundred bravest men to help you fight Yenibohor," announced Matsi calmly. "They're down below in the creek, on the rafts, with my father. . . . I insisted on coming, too. I so badly wanted to see you again!"

"Your people's assistance will be crucial for us, little girl," said Kushumai, ruffling Matsi's strange white hair. "I shall thank the Men of the Sea and speak to them in person. Meanwhile, go and tell them to wait, and above all, not to move — we haven't finished drawing up our battle plan."

Matsi nodded. She waved and shouted to Coral, as she wad-
dled off barefoot:

"See you later, Coral! See you later!"

"Wait for me, Matsi!" yelled Coral. "I'm coming with you!"

"Be careful!" Qadwan couldn't help shouting after her as she
vanished over the crest of the hill.

Kushumai turned to her army chiefs. Her green eyes were
shining.

"We haven't resolved the problem of the priests' magic powers, but now I know how we're going to enter the city."

≋ ✳ ≋ ✳ ≋

"Can you see them?" Godfrey whispered to Romaric, who had
crawled through the grass to eavesdrop on Kushumai explaining
her battle plan to her chiefs of staff.

"No," he whispered back. "But I can hear them! Shhh! Now
be quiet!"

When they woke up, Agatha, Godfrey, Romaric, and Toti had
learned of the arrival of the Men of the Sea, and that Coral
had rushed off to join them. They had tried, discreetly, to be part
of the meeting on the hilltop, but they had been firmly sent pack-
ing. Although Kushumai had had the tact to thank them for their
enthusiasm and their willingness, Yorwan had told them to "go
away and play."

That had infuriated the friends. These adults really were the
limit! They who had experience of the Uncertain World, who had
always found a way out of the worst situations, they who had ral-
lied the fierce Warriors of the Steppes and the devoted People of

the Sea, were now being politely told to "leave things up to the grown-ups and go away and play." It was so unfair! What ingratitude! They wanted to be part of the action. They would wait and see what happened.

Lying in the grass and making himself as inconspicuous as possible, Romaric pricked up his ears in the hope of overhearing what the adults were hatching. Kushumai was pointing with a stick to a spot on a drawing on the ground which of course he couldn't see.

"Once the gates are open, we have to get to this tower at all costs," she was saying. "That's where the High Priest of Yenibohor lives, and that must be where Robin is being held prisoner, there's no doubt about that."

"And in your view, where are the knights who survived the first attack being held?" asked Gerald.

"Most definitely here, in the city's dungeons," replied Kushumai, pointing to another place on the drawing. "We must take advantage of the battle to try and free them. The surviving knights would give our forces a huge boost."

"What about the priests?" enquired Yorwan. "What are we going to do?"

"I still don't know," admitted Kushumai. "My informers have counted around eight hundred Orks and one hundred and eighty priests. Although there are more than a thousand of us, we know it will be difficult to hold out against the monsters. And I fear that three sorcerers and one sorceress will not be enough to counter the priests' evil magic."

Her words dampened their spirits. Tofann was the first to speak:

"We will fight bravely! Battles and sacrifices are part of normal life in The Uncertain World!"

"I share your view, friend of the steppes," agreed the Hunter of the Purple Forest. "Death is merely a stage in the perpetual dance of the elements!"

"Oh, fine sentiments indeed," sneered the archer, whose face was disfigured by a deep scar. "I'm quite happy to fight, but I don't intend to get myself killed! So we'd better find a way of eliminating the sorcerer-priests."

"The archer's right," said the instrument-maker. "The men of the West are brave and they are prepared to fight so that they can live in freedom on their lands without having to pay the crushing taxes demanded by Yenibohor. But it would be unjust to ask them to sacrifice themselves in vain."

"The problem is that we don't really have a choice," said Gerald. "Each person here seems to have a good reason to fight, but these are personal reasons. What's at stake right now in Yenibohor goes beyond our own interests. If the evil hiding within these walls — be he The Shadow, High Priest, or whoever — succeeds in combining the powers of the book of spells he stole and those of the boy he has kidnapped, the consequences will be dire for everyone!"

Kushumai tried to calm the men, who became alarmed at the sorcerer's words.

"We have all day to find a solution," she declared. "In any case, we plan to attack tomorrow, at dawn. Gerald is right. We have no choice. And waiting is not an option."

≈ ✳ ≈ ✳ ≈

Romaric reported everything he had overheard to the others in Ska, so that Toti could understand.

"I had no idea the situation was so desperate," wailed Agatha. "What are we going to do?"

"I didn't hear everything," he replied. "But this is what I suggest. . . . Tomorrow, we agree to keep out of danger in the Gray Hills while the others attack Yenibohor. Then we quietly slip down and secretly enter the city. Then we'll have to try and find the tower where Robin's locked up. We make ourselves as unobtrusive as possible and we go there. After that, I don't know."

"Not bad," said Godfrey sarcastically. "There'll be time to decide when we get there, if we get there alive!"

"It could work, if we manage not to be spotted," ventured Toti.

"Have you got an alternative?" asked Romaric, upset. "No? well then . . ."

"What about Coral?" asked Agatha.

"She'll be back by then."

"And Thomas and Amber?" added Godfrey.

"I'm sure Amber will arrive in time," said Romaric calmly. "She'd never desert Robin. You know that as well as I do."

27
NEVER SAY DIE

The next day, as expected, Romaric and the others were politely asked to stay in the Gray Hills while preparations were made for battle.

"But we won't see a thing," protested Coral.

After spending the previous day with Wal and Matsi, she had joined her friends that evening and they had told her the latest developments. Qadwan walked over to them; the other adults seemed to have appointed him as their official spokesman for negotiating with the friends.

"Now, children . . . ," he said. "War is for adults. I know you're worried about Robin, but you've already done a lot for him. You must be reasonable."

Scowling, they hung their heads but made no objection. The elderly sorcerer took their attitude as resignation and turned on his heels, satisfied, unaware of the winks being exchanged behind his back.

≋　⚹　≋　⚹　≋

Flanked by Yorwan and Gerald, Kushumai was surveying the preparations being made by her troops, which she had nick-named "the army of the Hills." She had talked at great length with the People of the Sea the day before and drawn up a daring battle plan. The first stage of the operation relied entirely on Wal and his companions. She watched the Warriors of the Steppes idle away the time by play-fighting among themselves. She admired their strength, suppleness, and skill in combat, which for them was a way of life. She would happily have exchanged several hundred auburn-haired men for just a few dozen of these warriors. Not that she doubted the courage of the people of the West, but they were still farmers, more adept at handling the plough than the sword. The instrument-maker had been sent by the Bear Society to teach the farmers of this region that was par-ticularly hostile to Yenibohor to fight, and he had done so with astounding success. But they were no match for the powerful enemy awaiting them. Kushumai was more hopeful of the ban-dits; if they had survived the skirmishes against the Ork mercenaries so far, then they had a good chance of surviving this approaching battle. As for the huntsmen of the Purple Forest, they were brave and experienced and had fought against fierce Orks in the forest. But they were few in number. Kushumai sighed. If only she had a squadron of magicians to oppose the priests. Those of The Uncertain World were either charlatans or cowards who trembled with fear at the mere mention of the High Priest of Yenibohor.

"What are you thinking about, Kushumai?"

"I'm not thinking, Lord Sha. I'm praying! It's the only thing we can do."

Just then a murmur rippled through the ranks of the men of the West, who suddenly ran off yelling in all directions.

"What's going on?" Gerald asked in alarm.

The hunters instinctively gathered around Kushumai to protect her.

"Mirgi, Mirgi!" wailed a man in reply.

According to the legends of The Uncertain World, Mirgi were evil spirits that took on the form of grimacing gnomes.

"Whoa! Calm down, everyone! It's me! It's us!" shouted someone trying to make himself heard above the din.

"Bertram?" exploded Gerald in disbelief.

"Yes, it's Bertram! Tell these men to put their axes away and lower their swords or someone will get hurt. This is crazy!"

It took Gerald a while to convince the men of the West that the new arrivals were friends, not foes. He also had trouble convincing them that the creatures with the young sorcerer were not Mirgi.

"Bertram!"

Intrigued by the noise, Romaric, Agatha, Godfrey, and Coral had come running, followed by Toti. Overjoyed at being reunited with their friend, they greeted Bertram with vigorous handshakes and hugs. When they caught sight of the creatures accompanying him, their jaws dropped in amazement.

"Friends from Dashtikazar. Me very happy to see you again!"

"Kor Hosik!"

It was indeed Kor Hosik, the young Korrigan who had acted

as interpreter for King Kor Mehtar when the gang had been held captive in his palace at Boulegant.

The Korrigans — dark, hairy, wizened little creatures around thirty inches high — lived on the moors of The Lost Isle, where they cohabited peacefully, so to speak, with the humans.

Behind Kor Hosik stood a dozen or so other Korrigans who seemed even more stunted and hunched than usual. Their hair and fur were gray or even white. Their wide-brimmed hats, jackets, and traditional velvet pantaloons weren't the customary black, but red. And their iron shoes were very shiny and worn.

"When Amber talked about assembling our various friends, I felt stupid and useless," confessed Bertram to his friends and to the army chiefs who had come over and were staring at the envoys of the People of the Moors in astonishment. "Then I had a brainwave!"

"You went back to The Lost Isle and went to see the Korrigans?" exclaimed Coral, dumbfounded. "That's wild!"

"It took ages. I ran nearly all the way to the Howling Coast and I was lucky enough to come across a fisherman who agreed to take me to The Middle Island."

"And did you run all the way back here, too?" asked Coral.

"Of course! You know, the Korrigans are very energetic. Even when they're really old. I was the one who had trouble keeping up with them."

"Go on, Bertram," said Gerald. "We all want to hear the rest of your story. And you, Coral, stop interrupting with your questions."

"Well, knowing the awesome powers of the priests of Yenibohor, I said to myself that we could do with the help of some sorcerers," continued Bertram. "Unfortunately, one of The Shadow's spies has infiltrated the Guild and we can't rely on its help. So I asked myself where I could find some magicians. Among the Korrigans, of course! So I whizzed back to The Lost Isle and went straight to the moors. I eventually found the dolmen where the entrance to Boulegant is. I waited until a Korrigan appeared and asked for an audience with Kor Mehtar. You know how curious the Korrigans are. He agreed to see me at once. I explained the situation, making it clear what the implications would be for his people if The Shadow became too powerful. He was convinced and agreed to let me take his most experienced magicians as well as an interpreter to help us communicate. That's the whole story."

"You say he was convinced?" repeated Gerald, dubiously.

"How come he's allowed to ask questions and I'm not?" muttered Coral under her breath.

"Shut up!" snapped Romaric. "We're trying to listen!"

"Yes," said Bertram in answer to Gerald's question, turning rather red. "I managed to do a deal, a deal that . . ."

"Your friend make promise to my king," broke in the delighted Kor Hosik. "Your friend promise something in exchange for our help!"

"That's between Kor Mehtar and myself!" protested Bertram, glaring daggers at the Korrigan. "Anyway, the main thing is that I got back here in time with friends to help, isn't it?"

"You're right, young Bertram," said Kushumai with a warm smile. "And the help that you've brought may perhaps save us all. I've heard of the magic of the Korrigans. They use Oghams, which are said to be very powerful. And best of all, their magic is unknown in this World . . . the priests will be caught completely off guard."

She turned to Yorwan and Gerald.

"There you are! At last we have our squadron of magicians. You see . . . never say die!"

To the great relief of the men of the West, who found it hard to believe that these strange creatures weren't Mirgi, Kushumai invited the Korrigans to follow her to the hill for a final briefing.

Bertram stayed with his friends, who told him what they'd been up to during the last few days. They satisfied his curiosity about Kushumai and Lord Sha and filled him in on Amber and Thomas's absence and the latest developments, but didn't tell him about their planned rebellion.

"It's a real pain that you have to stay in these hills," said Bertram, knitting his brow and speaking in an assured voice that implied that he identified with the adults. "I'll be thinking of you when I'm in the thick of the fighting, between clashes with the Orks and bouts of magic against the priests. Anyway, looks as if I'm wanted. Be good! I'll try and make you proud of me," he ended, seeing Gerald coming toward him.

"Bertram?"

"Coming, Gerald. Farewell my friends, farewell . . ."

"Bertram," began Gerald awkwardly. "We need someone to keep an eye on . . . to protect your friends. Qadwan's feeling better. He's more experienced than you and will be more useful to us against the priests."

"What?" roared Bertram. "But Qadwan's senile; he'll be a nuisance! Gerald, you can't do this to me. . . . Please!"

"That's enough, I've made my decision," said the sorcerer in a tone that brooked no argument. "Just try to keep a closer eye on these young people than you did on The Lost Isle!"

Shocked and upset, Bertram watched him walk away. Gerald was on his way to join the other chiefs. The army of the Hills was preparing to march on the town.

"Come on, Bertram." Godfrey comforted him, teasing. "Don't worry, it'll be different when you grow up. . . ."

"Very funny! When I think of all I've done for them," he complained. "They have no right to exclude me. I deserve to take part in the battle!"

"That's how we all feel," said Romaric, placing a hand on the young sorcerer's shoulder. "And what's more, we have a plan."

"A plan? Don't tell me you're thinking of disobeying Gerald again . . . Oh no!"

"Oh yes, Bertram. Oh yes!"

28
WATER AND AIR

The advance of the army of the Hills caused quite a stir in the city of Yenibohor. There was panic even on the ramparts, where heavily armed Orks could be seen running to take up their positions.

Kushumai rapped out orders; her men halted and remained beyond the range of any arrows. They stood facing the main gate, which was firmly shut and looked capable of withstanding any attack.

"All we have to do is wait," Kushumai told her companions. "And above all, hope that the People of the Sea succeed."

The Foaming River ran through the center of the city and flowed into the Infested Sea. Transformed into a canal inside the city, it served a number of purposes and provided the only relief from the monotony of the buildings. It flowed into and out of Yenibohor, gliding under the ramparts through a barred vault. The river waters and those of the sea were home to huge flesh-eating fish that you wouldn't want to meet while bathing!

Ousnak, an outstanding huntsman who had been chosen unanimously by all the Tribes to lead this strange underwater expedition,
stopped swimming and turned around. His long white hair
streamed behind him. The hundred or so men that the People of
the Sea had dispatched to the aid of the army of the Hills followed
him in a compact group; they were accomplished underwater
swimmers. They had breathed in a supply of air and knew they
could hold out for many minutes by economizing their move-
ments. Satisfied, Ousnak set off again.

He soon spied the bars that stopped the sea monsters from
swimming up the river into the city. The membrane protecting
his eyes acted like a diving mask and he could make out the tiniest details of his surroundings. He quickly spotted the metal bar
that was eaten away by rust at the bottom where it touched the
seaweed-covered riverbed. That would be their way into the city.
Ousnak beckoned: Three men came to help him twist the rusty
bar. One by one the swimmers darted through the opening the men
had made. Cautiously coming up for air, they filled their lungs
again and plunged back down to the depths. Raising their heads to
breathe, they could see that the attention of the Orks and the priests
was completely focused on the plain where the attackers were gathered. Kushumai was right. The underwater commando unit was
guaranteed to catch the defenders off guard.

Ousnak checked that the knife he normally used to gut fish
was still in the belt of his loincloth. He stroked it to give himself
courage and motioned to the others to advance. They came to
the wide bridge that continued on from the main gate, and sheltered beneath it. The gate, a few dozen meters away, was guarded
by only two Orks. The others were positioned on the ramparts.

The rulers of Yenibohor clearly thought that the heavy wooden beam barring the two metal gates would deter any attackers.

"We are going to split into three groups," whispered Ousnak. "One will attack the Orks, the second will open the gate, and the third will cover our retreat."

The Men of the Sea silently clambered onto the bank. Ousnak extricated from his wide belt an object that Kushumai had given him when she had visited his raft the day before to inform him of her battle plan. He undid the waterproof wraps protecting it and pointed the metal barrel skyward. He did as the woman with green eyes had instructed him. He pressed a button to release a ball of fire into the air which exploded noiselessly in an intense flash of blue light.

"The signal!" exclaimed Kushumai on the other side of the walls. She had been anxiously scanning the sky for a while. "They've done it! They're going to try to open the gate. Be ready!"

Inside the city, the first group of Men of the Sea rushed at the Orks with the second group right behind them, while the third group fanned out between the gate and the bridge. The two Orks were so astonished to see a group of half-naked men brandishing knives appear out of nowhere that they were unable to offer much resistance. The first Ork was quickly overcome, but the other recovered his wits, felled two men, and yelled for his fellow Orks to come to his aid. Too late: The beam had been removed and the gates swung wide open.

"Forward!" roared Kushumai. "Into battle!"

Farmers from the West, bandits, hunters, and Warriors of the Steppes all charged.

Meanwhile, Ousnak's men, who had at last finished off the

second Ork, made their way back to the river, taking with them the bodies of the unfortunate men the monster had killed.

"We haven't done too badly," commented Wal, Matsi's father, nursing a bloody gash on his arm.

"No," agreed Ousnak. "But there is nothing more for us to do here. The People of the Sea have fulfilled their promise. Now it's up to others to do their part. We are not warriors."

The white-haired men dived silently into the river and swam back toward the sea.

The first to reach the city were the Warriors of the Steppes, followed by the Hunters of the Purple Forest led by Kushumai herself. They ran up against a dozen Orks who were struggling to shut the gates.

"At last, some action!" roared Tofann, bringing down his huge sword on the skull of one of the monsters, who was astounded to find himself confronted by someone his own size.

The warriors had slaughtered the Orks at the gate before the hunters even arrived.

"You could have saved us a few!" joked one of them, wielding a sword in one hand and an axe in the other.

"Don't worry, there are enough to go around," replied Tofann, jerking his chin to indicate the clusters of Orks pouring down from the ramparts.

"The others had better get a move on," said Kushumai anxiously. "What's keeping them?"

"I think there's a problem," said a hunter.

And there was. A hundred yards from the walls, bandits and men of the West who made up the bulk of the troops lay on the ground shouting in surprise and anger. They had come up against something fluid and milky that had knocked them over like bowling pins — a sort of giant magic wave that had flung them to the ground.

Kushumai looked up toward the top of the ramparts: The priests had woven a powerful spell that was preventing their friends from coming to their aid.

"Courage!" she cried to the fifty or so men who had closed ranks. "Yorwan and Gerald are outside with the Korrigan magicians. They're bound to find a solution!"

"And fast, I hope," said Tofann calmly. "Because it looks as though there's a huge number of Orks coming toward us!"

≈ ✳ ≈ ✳ ≈

Yorwan and Gerald knew there was no point relying on force alone to rescue Kushumai, trapped inside the city with only a handful of men. Brave as they were, they wouldn't last any longer than the knights at the hands of Thunku's hordes of Orks. The two sorcerers glared daggers at the white-robed priests forming a chain to project their magic from the top of the wall. Then they went into a huddle with Qadwan and the Korrigans.

"Gerald, Qadwan, and I will combine our powers," Yorwan explained to Kor Hosik. "Your magic is too different for us to join forces with you. Let the Korrigans do their best to help us destroy the white wave."

Kor Hosik reported back to the elderly sages. They nodded. The Korrigans drew a circle on the ground and began to dance in the center, while the three sorcerers held hands and adopted the Stadha of The Uncertain World to create a counter-spell.

By the power of the Auroch and the Hand, of the Swan and the

Year, Uruz who runs on the hard snow, Naudhiz who goes naked in the cold, Elhaz who crackles as it burns, Yera the generous, put the evil spirits to sleep and undo what the magic has done! UNEY!

Gar! Venomous as the snake,
violent spirit of the lake,
by the power of the silver birch,
and the blood that quenches your thirst,
destroy the powerful hex
that menaces your subjects!

The magic of the stars attacked the priests' spell. A golden haze wrestled with the translucent wave and tried to contain it, like a makeshift storm barrier. But after a struggle it gave way and exploded in a shower of yellow sparks.

Immediately behind, conjured up by the magic of the Korrigans, the power of the earth and the moon struck the wave with an intense red flash. The air went cloudy around the milky spell, which froze and then retreated a fraction. But although momentarily disrupted, the priests' protection held good.

"Us magic stronger than magic of men in white on big walls," lamented Kor Hosik. "But they too many. A bit less men in white and us smash the spell!"

"You're right, Kor Hosik," said Gerald gloomily. "But what can we do?"

There was a loud explosion. A priest swayed on the ramparts, then toppled forward and landed in a heap.

29

FIRE AND EARTH

"What was that?" asked Gerald, who had witnessed the scene.

Another detonation was heard and a second priest came hurtling down, clutching his stomach.

"Over there!" exclaimed Yorwan, pointing at the rocks from which Urian Penmarch had harangued the Brotherhood a few days earlier.

Some Men of the Sands were calmly sniping at the priests, the barrels of their antiquated rifles resting on the stones as they adjusted their sights. The three sorcerers ran to join the men wearing heavy midnight-blue, cream, and bloodred robes. Nobody had ever seen firearms in The Uncertain World and their long single-barreled shotguns caused some amazement among the bandits and the farmers of the West.

"Gerald!" cried Amber with a smile, running to meet him.

"Amber?" exclaimed Gerald, catching sight of her. "So you did it!"

"Yes," confirmed Amber in excitement. "When we got to the Ravenous Desert, Thomas and I lit a big fire to attract the attention of the Men of the Sands. They came, but it took forever. After that we had to find Robin's friend Kyle and tell him our story. Then Kyle had to assemble the three clans and persuade them to help us. Then we had to get back. All that took ages. That's why we've only just gotten here. And then . . ."

"Is your friend Thomas all right?" Qadwan asked suddenly. "Is he with you?"

"Yes, er . . . he . . . he's here. He's fine."

"Thomas?" called Qadwan, alarmed by Amber's hesitation. "Where are you hiding?"

"I'm not hiding," said Thomas.

He emerged from the shelter of the rocks followed by Romaric, Godfrey, Bertram, Coral, Agatha, Toti, and a boy of their age, with blue eyes, black hair, and a tanned complexion.

"No!" exclaimed Gerald when he saw the whole gang. "Bertram, didn't I ask you to . . . ?"

"I tried," Bertram protested. "But they're a hot-headed bunch!"

"We needed guides to find you," interrupted the dark-haired boy.

He introduced himself.

"I'm Kyle, and I am the son of the chiefs of the three Tribes of the Desert."

"Kyle, welcome to you and to the brave Men of the Sands," replied Yorwan, before Gerald could say another word. "I must say that although the Men of the Sands' rifles are somewhat ancient, they're certainly effective!"

"My people have always had firearms — well, since they've been stuck in the Ravenous Desert," Kyle began to explain. "They probably came from another World, where we must have acquired them when we lived as nomads. For generations, the rifle has passed from father to son. We take great care of them for they protect us from bandits, the occupants of Yadigar, and from the Desert."

"What amazes me," mused Gerald, "is that the bullets are not repelled by the magic wave as we are."

"I think they're too fast for the priests' magic," replied Yorwan, after thinking for a moment. "The main thing is that they work! The fewer priests there are, the weaker the spell will be. Let's go back to the Korrigans and prepare to force our way through."

Gerald agreed. Before setting out, Yorwan turned to the young people, frowned, and put on a severe expression.

"I absolutely forbid you to leave these rocks! If I see one of you disobey my order, I promise you a punishment you won't forget for the rest of your life! I hope I've made myself clear."

≈ ✳ ≈ ✳ ≈

Meanwhile Kushumai, her hunters, and the Warriors of the Steppes were being attacked by the Orks swarming down from the ramparts.

The young woman unsheathed her sword and pointed it confidently at the charging monsters. The hunters gathered around her, ready to lay down their lives to defend her. The warriors dispersed to give themselves more freedom of movement.

"The first to arrive in the Steppes of Light wait for the others!" yelled Tofann almost joyfully to his companions.

An Ork pounced on him, wielding a bloodstained club. The giant grabbed his mighty sword with both hands and easily fended off the attack. Then he bent down and wheeled around, attacking the Ork viciously. He nimbly sidestepped an attack by another monster from behind, landed him a kick that had the Ork bent double, surrendering.

"I've always said that Orks were less dangerous than they seemed!" quipped Tofann, who looked as though he was enjoying himself.

The hunters wouldn't have agreed with him. They were having a difficult time containing the monsters, and three of their number had already been killed. Luckily, experienced in the techniques of group fighting, the hunters had set up a defensive line made up of swordsmen who somehow managed to keep the furious Orks at bay.

"If your sorcerers don't polish off the priests soon, we're going to be overwhelmed," warned one of the hunters.

"I know," replied Kushumai, getting her breath back. "How are the warriors of the North doing?"

"They seem to be giving the enemy a hard time," replied a hunter admiringly.

The Huntress was thankful for the warriors' presence. They were outstanding fighters. A hundred of them could conquer The Uncertain World. Luckily, they were a nomadic people, owning no land, and although they earned their living fighting, they had no wish to subdue and control other tribes.

There was a glint of fear in the Orks' tiny, cruel eyes as they took on the strapping warriors. Many of them lay on the ground, whereas the giants of the North were all still on their feet.

"Hey ho apple pie, one in the chest and one in the eye!" boomed Tofann, felling one Ork.

"Hey ho baked beans, we'll smash you all to smithereens!" chorused his companions, cutting a swathe through the terrible Orks.

They were all so absorbed in the battle going on inside the city that nobody noticed the priests keeling over on the ramparts.

The Men of the Sands aimed methodically, taking their time, and each shot hit home. The priests stationed on top of the city's high wall looked at each other in sheer terror. But at the risk of destroying the spell that was keeping the army of the Hills away from the city, they couldn't move. Ghostly pale, they watched their fellow priests being picked off one by one.

"Now our magic should work," declared Yorwan, looking pleased as he counted the white forms on the ramparts. "Come on, let's give it another go."

But Kor Hosik stepped in.

"The Korrigan sages say you let earth magic work. White wave no strong now."

Yorwan, Gerald, and Qadwan wavered and finally agreed so as not to offend their allies. After all, there would be plenty of time to call on the magic of the stars if the Korrigans' spells didn't work.

The elderly Korrigans began their dance again, humming a spell in Korrigani as the sorcerers looked on fascinated.

"Stann! Bone of the earth,
power of the deep and of Eternity,
by the power of the ethereal flame,

and the stone dragon,
turn into a raging sea
against a raging sea!
Advance and destroy the barricade!"

The red magic oozed out from the circle on the ground.

It formed into a giant wave that rolled toward the white wave protecting the city. Although weakened by the deaths of so many priests, the milky energy wave still managed to rise up and combat the Korrigans' magic. But when the red magic blade crashed into it with a thunderous roar, it shattered and meekly dispersed.

"Attack!" yelled the archer, rushing toward Yenibohor.

The bandits were hot on his heels.

"Attack!" cried the instrument-maker, calling the men of the West to battle.

"Shall we go?" Yorwan asked his companions.

"Let's go!" chorused Gerald and Qadwan.

From the rock where Gerald had confined them, the young friends watched the armies set off to attack Yenibohor. Even the Korrigans joined the group. Despite their diminutive height, they ran faster than anyone else. Soon the Men of the Sands joined the bandits, too.

Coral turned away for a moment. She had been appalled by the horrific violence taking place in the city, and she was troubled by the thought that many of the brave warriors now going into battle would also die horribly. Then she squared her shoulders: There was no going back.

Amber watched the Huntress admiringly. No one would believe

from her cool manner that she was leading an army into battle against a terrible fate. Amber frowned, thinking hard. It was strange; she felt as if she'd seen the Huntress somewhere before.

As the army drew near the gates, the nine youngsters exchanged looks.

"Should we stay put like good boys and girls?" asked Godfrey sarcastically.

"Are you kidding?" replied Kyle.

"Yorwan said that he didn't want to see a single one of us leave the rock," recalled Romaric. "But supposing we all leave together? We wouldn't really be disobeying!"

"It's true. Romaric's right!" said Coral.

Oddly, Bertram didn't try and reason with him. He even seemed more impatient than the others.

"So what are we waiting for?" he asked.

"Last one into the city's a chicken!" cried Amber.

They raced toward the high walls, yelling like wild animals.

30

THE NOOSE TIGHTENS

"Master! Master! The army outside is preparing to invade the city."

The shadowy form stood before a solid oak table in the middle of the room that served as his laboratory at the top of the Tower. A thick book with a black binding studded with stars lay open before him and he was reading it feverishly.

He turned menacingly toward the priest who had interrupted him.

"You dare disturb me . . . for a trifling matter . . ."

The man with a shaved head and white tunic groveled.

"But, Master . . . ," he stammered.

"Discuss these details with Lomgo and Thunku. I pay them enough for that. . . . Now, enough! I forbid anybody to disturb me again. Even if the city were to fall into the sea. . . ."

The priest fell silent and fled from the room without arguing. Too bad, the Master wouldn't know that Lomgo had disappeared into thin air since the city had been under siege.

The Shadow returned to the spell contained in the *Book of the Stars*. It was one of the last ones he had managed to decode, using all his powers. The rest of the Book remained obstinately inaccessible to him.

One of the peculiarities of the *Book of the Stars*, which was the source of the Guild's magic knowledge, was that it appeared to have a will of its own. Despite the sorcerers' persistent efforts and the determination of The Shadow himself, the Book would not allow the reader to go beyond a certain page. And that was how it had been for centuries. It had taken The Shadow some fierce battles with the *Book of the Stars* to finally extract some fragments of spells . . . which he alone now knew.

But what use were these tiny fragments compared with all the promises contained in its pages? The person who succeeded in deciphering the entire Book would dominate the whole World, would dominate all the Worlds! The person who mastered the *Book of the Stars* would be able to subjugate The Lost Isle, The Uncertain World and, above all, The Real World.

It required little to achieve this. Just a certain boy with an exceptionally developed Ond who was more receptive than others to the powers of the Graphems. And that very boy was there, in a cell in the basement of the Tower, but for some unaccountable reason The Shadow had been unable to persuade him to cooperate.

The Shadow banged his fist down on the table in frustration, then forced himself to concentrate once more on his spell.

He had an idea for overcoming Robin's resistance. An idea that had demanded all his time and energy since the fiasco of his last attack.

Since confronting the boy directly only seemed to reinforce his powers, The Shadow had decided on a surprise attack, to catch him unawares. So, from his table he had woven a complicated spell which he distilled unseen through the walls of the tower, Graphem after Graphem. The first effects were beginning to appear as Robin sat in his cell, motionless at the center of his cosmic sphere in the ecstatic pose that isolated him from the outside world. The bluish light of Odala no longer illuminated the Armor of Egishjamur and the red flames were extinguished on three of the eight branches of Hagal.

≈ ✳ ≈ ✳ ≈

The violence of the army's attack forced the Orks to retreat to the bridge over the river. Kushumai stood in the midst of the crush, scanning the scene for the leaders of the army of the Hills, so as to organize operations in the city. Her green eyes blazed. She was magnificent, standing proud as a war goddess.

"Hunters! To the prison!" she cried, rallying her men. "Free the knights locked up inside!"

The men of the Purple Forest rushed toward the building that housed the jails of Yenibohor, according to the Bear Society's spies.

"Archer! Instrument maker! Take care of the Orks!" Kushumai commanded.

The battle raged. The men of the West were having trouble standing up to the monsters. The bandits were faring better, but it was clear that the odds were against them.

"We'll do our best!" yelled the archer.

Kushumai, who had not lost sight of the main objective of

the attack, ensured that Yorwan, Gerald, and Qadwan and the Korrigans were close behind her. The Tower probably had its own defense force constituted not of Orks, but of priests.

"Tofann! We're going to the Tower," she called. "Get your warriors to clear us a path!"

"You did say clear a path?" replied the giant. "Very well!"

He leaped forward and felled an Ork with one blow.

Gerald looked away. The violence all around them sickened him, making him still more determined to defeat their merciless enemy.

The Warriors of the Steppes used their huge swords to cut a path straight through the battlefield. The sorcerers, Korrigans, and Men of the Sands with their ancient guns fell in behind them, fleet as shadows.

≋ ✳ ≋ ✳ ≋

"The Tower! Isn't that the tower you escaped from?" Agatha asked Romaric.

"I don't see any other tower," he replied teasingly.

The little gang had managed to slip inside the city and, taking advantage of the general pandemonium and the clouds of dust thrown up by the fighting, had found sanctuary on a little side street, away from the battle.

"Let's go there," suggested Amber. "No point wasting time."

"I agree," said Bertram.

The nine youngsters set off in the direction of the dark Tower silhouetted against the sky. They were careful to keep to the back streets and to stay close to the walls.

They were nearing the foot of the Tower when Coral screamed. Emerging from an adjoining street, an Ork was preparing to chase them, whirling his club above his head.

"Oh, no!" groaned Amber.

"Don't you feel as though we've done this all before?" exclaimed Godfrey with a sigh.

He had just been reminded of the episode in Penmarch Forest when they had been ambushed by Orks.

"Definitely," retorted Thomas. "Watch me!"

He unsheathed the hunting knife borrowed from Agatha's father and spun around. Then he rushed forward to meet the Ork, who clearly had not been expecting to be attacked. The monster barely had the time to bring down his club on Thomas before toppling over and crumpling to the ground, propelled by his own momentum. Thomas, wounded in the leg and on the shoulder, screamed in terror. Tears of pain welled up in his eyes, but he somehow found the strength to stab the Ork with his knife before passing out. Beneath him, the Ork struggled for a moment, then was still.

"Thomas!"

Agatha raced over to her friend. The rest of the gang followed. They tried to take care of Thomas, who lay unconscious. But none of them had the faintest idea what to do. Seeing his companions' awkwardness and confusion, Toti quickly rolled the injured Thomas onto his side to stop him from choking.

"Do you know about first aid?" asked Agatha, looking hopefully at the boy.

"I'm the one who takes care of my brother's friends when they're wounded," Toti told her, blushing faintly.

"In that case, if you don't mind, you can help me get Thomas to safety in one of these empty houses," suggested Agatha. "The rest of you, go to the Tower. It's right in front of us!"

Romaric, Coral, Amber, Godfrey, and Bertram hated to abandon them, but they recognized that Agatha was right. They had to see their mission through to the end. Otherwise, all they had done so far would be in vain.

"Good luck, Agatha," said Amber, hugging her.

"Save Robin for me!" replied Agatha, moved. "And please keep an eye on Godfrey," she added softly.

Amber gazed at Agatha in disbelief, then gave a little smile to show she had got the message. Female secrets.

She placed herself at the head of the group now down to six, and a few minutes later they entered the Tower through a half-open postern.

31

THE KNIGHTS MAKE

A COMEBACK

The roar of battle had reached the ears of the knights imprisoned in the dungeons of Yenibohor. Some gave their comrades a leg up to see if they could glimpse what was happening through the high, barred windows looking out onto the street.

"We can't see a thing," Ambor said, astride the Commander's shoulders.

"The noise seems to be coming from the city gates," said Quadehar, sitting on Urian's shoulders in the neighboring cell. "I think it must be the reinforcements that Gerald and Qadwan have brought from The Lost Isle," he added hopefully.

Joyful shouts echoed in the corridor between the two rows of cells.

"If Master Quadehar is right, we must be prepared — our companions will try to free us!" boomed the Commander.

But the knights were already on their feet ready for action, awaiting their rescuers with renewed hope and strength.

A commotion, accompanied by stifled cries, was soon heard coming from the guards' room. The knights, who were expecting to see other knights brought in from The Lost Isle by Gerald, were amazed to see men sporting strange purple armor and helmets crowned with animal skulls charging along the corridor. They were all the more astonished when these men opened the doors to their cells with keys they'd taken from the guards and spoke to them in the language of The Uncertain World.

"How many are you?" asked one of the rescuers.

"There are a hundred and twenty of us," replied the Commander, identifying himself. "A hundred and twenty knights including forty who are slightly wounded."

"If they can hold a sword, even the injured will be welcome," declared the hunter. "We've got to go and help the untrained fighters at the city gates. The Orks are decimating them!"

"Untrained?" queried Bertolen, surprised.

"Bandits and poor farmers from all over The Uncertain World! People more used to cutting corn than slitting throats, more skilled at robbing merchants than confronting bloodthirsty monsters!"

"Did you hear?" the Commander asked his men. "Are we going to allow poor people to be massacred, people who have had the courage and kindness to come to the help of visitors from another World?"

"No!" the knights shouted in unison.

"Where can we find weapons?" asked the Commander, turning to the hunter.

"There are Orks' sabers and axes in the guards' room."

"I think that'll do us just fine," said Ambor.

≈ ✳ ≈ ✳ ≈

Meanwhile, near the entrance to the city, trapped between the main gate and the Foaming River, the men of the West and the bandits had suffered heavy losses. Despair was written on the fighters' faces as they parried and returned the blows, knowing all was lost.

The Orks, on the other hand, grunted with satisfaction as the ranks of the army of the Hills became depleted. They figured that it wouldn't take long to polish off these doomed forces.

Suddenly, there was the sound of a stampede. The Orks closest to the bridge turned around, their beady eyes wild with panic. An entire company of knights brandishing toothed sabers and sharp axes had rushed out of the street leading to the prison and was poised to attack them.

"We're saved!" yelled the archer.

"Knights of The Lost Isle! It's the knights of The Lost Isle!" cried the instrument maker.

Inspired by the arrival of these unexpected reinforcements, the bandits and farmers threw themselves into the battle with renewed energy.

Charging heads down and arms raised into the midst of the petrified Orks, the knights vented their fury, a fury increased by the humiliation of their time in prison. Now the tables had turned and the Orks slowly began to retreat.

Urian and Quadehar, who was still wearing poor Valentino's

battered armor, were the last to come out of the prison. The giant entreated his friend to hurry; the knights were already far ahead and it sounded as if the first were already confronting the Orks, from the cries that reached their ears. But the sorcerer was looking elsewhere, toward the evil tower rising up in the center of the city.

"Never mind the knights; there are enough of them. We've got more important things to do."

"More important than fighting?" protested Urian. "But, Quadehar . . ."

"Listen to me, Urian!" said the sorcerer curtly. "Don't you think you've made enough mistakes already?"

The giant hung his head, suddenly reminded that Valentino's death was all his fault. His shoulders slumped and a tear rolled down his cheek.

"I'm sorry, Quadehar," apologized Urian in a small voice. "I behaved like a madman."

"Being sorry's no use. We've got to get to the Tower. I'm sure that's where Robin's being held."

Without another word, Quadehar swung around and hurried toward the menacing building, dragging Lord Penmarch behind him.

≈ ✳ ≈ ✳ ≈

"What's the plan?" Kyle asked his friends, once they were all inside the tower.

"We look for Robin and we get him out of here!" replied Bertram.

"In a nutshell," agreed Godfrey.

The room they were in looked like a kitchen. They must have come in through a tradesmen's entrance. Luckily it was empty, perhaps evacuated hurriedly as the overturned chairs and the gaping door suggested. A corridor opposite led to a spiral staircase that went down to the basement and up to the other floors.

As they were about to go up the staircase, the sound of footsteps had them scurrying back down again.

"Someone's coming!" exclaimed Coral in a whisper.

"We must hide!" said Romaric.

"Where?" asked Coral, looking desperately around.

"There, in the cupboard!" suggested Kyle.

The six of them rushed over to a huge cupboard that ran the length of the wall and piled inside. Luckily, the cupboard — probably a huge pantry — was completely empty. They pulled the door closed behind them, but were careful to leave it open a fraction.

Some fifty Orks came thundering into the kitchen. More terrifying than all those they had seen so far, they were led by a monstrous giant in black armor whose eyes blazed angrily. The Orks were followed by three priests with shaved skulls, dressed in their habitual white tunics.

A shudder of terror ran through the little gang hidden in the cupboard.

"Thunku!" murmured Coral.

"Shhh!" hissed Amber, rolling her eyes.

The Orks and their chief, who was indeed Commander Thunku, left the Tower. The priests carefully shut the main door behind them, cast a rapid spell to lock it tight, then silently moved off.

The young friends waited awhile with pounding hearts before daring to leave their hiding place.

≈ ✳ ≈ ✳ ≈

"Good heavens! What's that?" exclaimed Urian, catching sight of a curtain of black flames barring the way to the Tower.

"A magic barrier created by the priests, most likely," explained Quadehar, examining the spell intently. "It's very solid. I won't be able to destroy it on my own."

He clenched his fists in rage.

"It's too bad!" stormed the sorcerer. "Robin's here, a few steps away, and I am completely powerless. Me, the Guild's best sorcerer! This is so infuriating. . . ."

"Modest as ever, I see, Quadehar," said a voice behind him.

Quadehar spun around. Gerald was standing in front of him, accompanied by a band of warriors.

"Don't worry," went on Gerald, while Quadehar gave him an emotional hug. "You're not alone. I promise you we'll get your apprentice out of there."

Tearing himself away from Quadehar's embrace, Gerald gave the introductions:

"Meet Tofann and his warriors from the steppes. Without his valiant men, we'd all have been dead by now."

Urian's face lit up on seeing the proud fighters.

"And this is Kor Hosik, sent by Kor Mehtar, the king of the Korrigans on The Lost Isle, accompanied by the great magicians of the Little People," continued Gerald, who was trying to perform the introductions properly.

"Most honored, I'm sure,
to be standing before
magicians of such repute!
Their skills I salute,"

said Quadehar in Korrigani, bowing respectfully. His gesture was greeted by murmurs of satisfaction from the Korrigans.

"Behind us are the Men of the Sands who, despite their guns, are as shy and retiring as ever. And this young woman behind Yorwan is the leader of our army and head of the Bear Society, which I'll tell you about later."

Kushumai took a step forward and gazed into Quadehar's eyes. Green eyes met gray, hers glistening with emotion, his wide in disbelief.

"You?" exclaimed the sorcerer, stunned.

"Hello, Azhadar, or rather Quadehar, since that seems to be your real name. I'm pleased to see you again. It's been such a long time. . . ."

32

UP AGAINST THE WALL

"You...er...know each other?" asked Yorwan, visibly flabbergasted.

He wasn't the only one. Gerald and Qadwan looked equally shocked.

"Er...yes," stammered Quadehar, turning a deep red and squirming in his armor. "We met, a few years ago, in a tavern in Ferghana...."

"You're turning bright red!" exclaimed Gerald. "It's the first time I've ever seen you like this!"

"It must be the heat," said Qadwan mischievously.

"So, are you called Azhadar?" asked Urian.

"Azhadar is the name our friend uses when he travels in The Uncertain World," replied Gerald, "so that he can carry out his investigations unhindered..."

"...and lead a double life," teased Qadwan.

"Oh, please," snapped Quadehar, irritated. "We happened to spend a few days together, that's all!"

"A few days and a few nights, actually," broke in Kushumai, who seemed amused at the sorcerer's discomfort.

"We were young. We met . . . fifteen years ago!"

"Fourteen," Kushumai corrected him. "Azhadar, why try to justify yourself? The past belongs to the past. Today I am Kushumai the Huntress, sorceress in exile in the Purple Forest, Chief of the Bear Society, and leader of the army which is about to take this city. And you are Quadehar, a Sorcerer of the Guild. Our paths have crossed again . . . not so that we can reminisce over the past, but so that we can save a child from The Lost Isle. And put an end, once and for all, to the scheming priests and their reign of terror in this World."

Quadehar stared at Kushumai. He had first met her during a mission he had been carrying out for the Guild in The Uncertain World. He remembered the brazen young girl who had danced on the tables of the taverns. He'd been besotted with her when he was a young sorcerer. This remarkable young girl had grown into a magnificent woman, with an impressive sense of assurance and determination.

Quadehar struggled to get a grip on himself.

"You are right, of course," he replied. "Let's get back to this wall of flames. How do we get through it?"

Yorwan pointed to the group of motionless priests on top of the tower, indicating that once again they were up against the magic of Bohor.

"We'll do as we have just done to get inside the city!" he replied to Quadehar. "We'll overpower them."

The Men of the Sands took up their positions at the base of

the Tower, raised their guns, and started to pick off the men in white, one by one.

At the same time, the Korrigans drew a circle in the dust, and the Warriors of the Steppes prepared to leap through the breach that would soon be opened up by the red magic.

Meanwhile, in his laboratory, The Shadow was jubilant. Robin's defenses had finally given way. The spell taken from the *Book of the Stars* and woven with infinite patience had defeated the Graphems surrounding the apprentice sorcerer.

The Shadow closed the book of spells. Trailing darkness behind him, he headed toward the staircase and hurried down to the floor where Robin was imprisoned. He opened the door: All the barriers between him and the boy seemed to have disintegrated and the boy lay on the floor, on the spot where the stellar sphere had smashed.

"At last . . . at last I shall be able to accomplish my life's work. . . ."

The Shadow approached Robin, who was moving weakly.

"You're waking up . . . good. That will save me having to wake you . . . too harshly. . . ."

"The . . . the Graphems?" stammered Robin hoarsely.

"Gone . . . vanished . . . destroyed . . . I told you that you'd be mine in the end."

The apprentice sorcerer tried to stand up and face his enemy. But he was much too weak and he collapsed onto the flagstone floor of his cell. The Shadow caught him. Robin felt an insidious cold seep into his body.

"I'm taking you to meet your destiny . . . our destiny. . . ."

Robin realized that The Shadow was carrying him, dragging

him, out of the room. He mustered his little remaining strength and let out a howl of protest, a howl of despair.

≈ ✳ ≈ ✳ ≈

The friends had finally summoned up the courage to leave their hiding place and head for the stairs. Now they couldn't decide whether to go up or down.

"I suggest we go down," said Bertram. "Robin's been taken prisoner, so he'll be in a cell. And everyone knows that cells are in the basement."

Nobody objected.

Romaric grabbed a lighted torch from a wall holder and led the way. Romaric, Bertram, and Godfrey descended into the bowels of the tower.

Coral dropped to her knees.

"Coral, what are you doing? The others already left!" urged Amber impatiently.

"It's OK, I'm coming. What's the hurry?" Coral replied, calmly lacing up her shoelaces.

Just then, a scream rang out above them.

"Did you hear that?"

"It sounded like Robin!"

Amber and Coral froze and strained their ears. All they could hear were regular, sharp shots from the guns outside.

"It was Robin, I tell you," repeated Amber. "Come on!"

"Amber, wait! We must tell the others!"

But her hot-headed sister was already tearing up the stairs.

"Why is it always the same?" moaned Coral, trailing behind.

They ran past one room, which was empty, climbed to the

next floor, and eventually came to a vast chamber cluttered with sorcery instruments.

Amber stood stock-still, trembling and pointing at something in the center of the chamber.

"There . . . look! It's Robin and . . ."

"The Shadow!"

Coral screamed at the sight that met her eyes.

Robin was lying on a huge table beside a fat book with a star-studded cover; he appeared to be moving feebly. Before the table stood a figure enveloped in shadows. As it turned to face the intruders, shreds of darkness fell to the floor with an ominous sizzling sound. Boring through the obscure shroud of darkness, two eyes began to glow like embers.

"Oh, how touching. . . . These young ladies must be your friends, boy. . . . Very good, very good . . . a spectacle needs spectators. An historic moment requires . . . witnesses. . . ."

The Shadow had spoken in a honeyed, almost soft voice, and his coaxing whispers made the twins' blood run cold. Terrified, incapable of retreating, they felt their legs turn to jelly and their hearts miss a beat. The Shadow snickered.

≈ ✳ ≈ ✳ ≈

"This is taking too long," complained Quadehar, removing his armor.

"Patience, my friend," replied Gerald. "The Men of the Sands are working as fast as they can!"

Just then, as if to confirm his words, two priests fell from the top of the tower. Reckoning that the number of defenders had been sufficiently reduced, the Korrigan sorcerers launched into their spell. Suddenly their magic rose up from the circle and began to attack the curtain of fire, scattering it in a burst of red and black droplets. The shock caused the remaining priests to collapse as if struck by lightning.

"At last!" exclaimed Quadehar.

The Warriors of the Steppes were making ready to storm the tower when a breathless hunter came running out of a side street.

"There's trouble at the gate! Thunku has arrived with more Orks, and there aren't enough knights to fight them. We need the help of the warriors of the North. And the priests are back in action. They're casting spells from the ramparts and paralyzing our men!"

Kushumai quickly assessed the situation. If the army of the Hills yielded to the Orks, they still wouldn't have time to invade the Tower. She made her decision:

"Tofann and his warriors will go with you; so will the Men of the Sands and the Korrigans, if they agree. I need the others here. It's the best I can do. I hope that the strength of the warriors, the skill of the Men of the Sands, and the Korrigans' powers will be sufficient to tip the balance in our favor."

Tofann agreed and so did Kor Hosik, acting as spokesman for the Korrigans. The Men of the Sands contented themselves with a nod of approval. Then they all rushed after the hunter.

Urian stepped forward.

"Kushumai, Quadehar, I request the honor of accompanying these brave men to assist my companions. Give me the chance to redeem myself. Let me join them."

"Go, elderly knight," consented the young woman after a moment's thought. "You are a warhorse, a hand-to-hand fighter.

Who knows what evil awaits us in this tower? There are forces at work that are outside your province. Go!"

Urian Penmarch shot the Huntress a look full of gratitude as he raced off toward the battlefield.

"Now we're really up against the wall, forgive the pun!" said Kushumai wryly.

"Huh! There's an old proverb on The Lost Isle that says you're most likely to find the mason at the foot of a wall," said Gerald with a smile of complicity. "We'll find the sorcerer in the Tower!"

Quadehar, Gerald, Qadwan, Kushumai, and Lord Sha stepped resolutely toward the main entrance to the Tower.

33

POWERLESS

As the sorcerers expected, the main door was locked and barred by a spell. Quadehar went to try his luck with a side door he'd spotted a little farther away.

"That's locked, too," he announced, coming back to the others.

"Too bad. Let's try and open this one," said Yorwan.

They combined their powers to invoke Elhaz, the unlocking Graphem. The door gave way more easily than they had anticipated.

"Between the five of us, we can really shift things," crowed Gerald.

"I think it's more likely that the priests who cast the spell were in a hurry," replied Kushumai. "Let's go. . . ."

Just then, they heard shouts behind them: A group of priests was making a beeline for the Tower.

"Where have they come from?" grumbled Quadehar.

"Probably from the ramparts," replied Kushumai. "They've come to give their colleagues a helping hand."

"Go on," urged Lord Sha. "Search the Tower! I'll hold them off."

"Are you sure?"

"Yes, Huntress. Go."

Lord Sha took up a terrifying stance and greeted the priests with a barrage of powerful Thursaz. The priests shouted angrily but were forced to stop to cast a defense spell.

"Go!" repeated the sorcerer.

Without further ado, Quadehar, Kushumai, Gerald, and Qadwan disappeared inside the building.

≈ ✳ ≈ ✳ ≈

At the top of the Tower, in the gray stone room crammed with furniture and strange instruments, Amber was the first to recover her wits. Once over her initial terror, she took a gulp of air, then as if propelled by some superhuman force, started moving toward the table where Robin was lying.

"Stay where you are! I spoke of a spectacle . . . and neither you nor your friend are among the actors. . . . Mere spectators, I said, mere spectators . . . If either of you dares to approach or tries to disturb my ritual . . . I shall turn you into a toad."

The Shadow's hollow whisperings rang out authoritatively. Robin was at this creature's mercy. Amber stopped dead, overwhelmed by a feeling of helplessness and a deep sense of injustice. Tears welled up in her eyes.

Behind her, Coral shared her distress.

They slowly retreated to the top steps of the staircase. They were so fascinated by what they were witnessing that it didn't occur to them to run away.

The Shadow suddenly stopped paying any attention to them, as if they didn't exist, and concentrated once more on the ritual he was about to enact with Robin and the book of spells. Amber and Coral tried to breathe normally and stop trembling with fear.

"Look, Amber! What's The Shadow doing to Robin?"

The Shadow had opened the *Book of the Stars* and was trying to revive his prisoner.

"It looks as though Robin's too weak to take part in his ritual."

"Don't you think we should try and get a bit closer, without his noticing?"

The Shadow suddenly swiveled his glowing eyes to look at them. They huddled in the doorway.

"Silence! Silence, wretched girls. I'm warning you . . . you're ruining my concentration. . . ."

"Good!" said Amber between gritted teeth.

They kept quiet. Without further consultation, they started to do as Coral had suggested and gradually inched toward Robin.

"You take me for an idiot," hissed The Shadow. "But there are two people here who really are idiots and are asking to be turned into toads. . . ."

The twins stopped a few steps from the door, realizing they had gone too far.

≋ ✳ ≋ ✳ ≋

"Suppose we bump into The Shadow around a bend in the staircase?" Bertram asked Romaric, who was gingerly picking his way down the steps, lighting the way with his torch.

"We jump on him and pull his ears!" said Godfrey sarcastically.

"Are you afraid, Bertram?" asked Kyle in surprise. "You're the one who suggested going down to the basement in the first place."

Bertram muttered something incomprehensible and grew silent.

The staircase seemed to go on forever, down and down. The walls were oozing with damp. In some places, huge spiders lay in wait at the centers of their webs.

Godfrey shuddered. "These spiders look as though they're fed on rats! It's odd that we haven't heard Coral scream yet. Coral?"

No answer. Godfrey anxiously asked everyone to wait.

"Who was the last one to see Coral?"

There was an awkward silence. They had each been thinking only of themselves as they'd made their way down the slippery stairs, so terrified were they at the thought of bumping into something nasty. Romaric passed the torch to Bertram, who was at the back. There were only four of them.

"Amber? Coral?" shouted Godfrey again.

"Maybe they got delayed," suggested Kyle.

"Or something's happened to them," said Godfrey gloomily.

"We're going back up!" said Romaric, placing himself at the head of the group again.

≋ ✳ ≋ ✳ ≋

Absorbed in his ritual, The Shadow picked up a vial containing a thick, murky liquid. He removed the stopper and slipped the vial between Robin's lips. The boy lay pale as death.

"Drink! Regain your strength . . . I need a live boy for the ritual, not a corpse. . . ."

Robin coughed and spat out some of the liquid. He suddenly

felt himself come back to life, as if he had been whipped. His body regained sufficient strength for him to be able to painfully sit up on the edge of the wooden table.

"Good. Very good, boy . . . now we can get down to business. . . ."

Suddenly, there was the sound of a stampede. The Shadow turned his terrifying gaze toward the two girls. Amber and Coral widened their eyes and raised their hands to show that it was nothing to do with them.

A shape appeared in the doorway, soon followed by two others. The Shadow let out a cry of anger. For there stood Quadehar, Gerald, and Kushumai, ready to march into the laboratory. On the stairs below, Qadwan was wheezing and trying to get his breath back.

The Shadow waved his arms in the direction of the door and shouted a few crude words.

"Master Quadehar!" exclaimed Coral.

"You!" exclaimed Quadehar, spotting the two girls huddled against the wall, a few paces away.

"What on earth are you doing here, and where are the others?" asked Gerald in surprise.

"They saw the light on and they came in . . . ," replied Kushumai with a shrug, before the twins could say anything. "Don't you think these questions can wait until later?"

Coral smiled at her gratefully. Explaining their presence would have been tricky. She winked at Amber, but her twin was staring at Kushumai as if she couldn't take her eyes off her.

Quadehar marched over to the table in the center of the room where Robin lay next to the *Book of the Stars*. But he didn't get far: The Shadow had erected a wall of energy just in front of the door, a barrier as transparent as glass but solid as steel.

Amber and Coral ran up to the invisible wall and touched it. They were prisoners! Separated from the sorcerer by The Shadow's magic. Quadehar's fingers were only a couple inches from theirs, but as unreachable as if they had been miles away.

The sorcerers and sorceress put their heads together.

"Get away from that wall!" Quadehar ordered the girls.

They obeyed at once.

Meanwhile, oblivious to the sorcerers, The Shadow was embarking on the ritual that would harness Robin's powers to enable him to penetrate the *Book of the Stars* and discover all its secrets.

Kushumai, Quadehar, and Gerald attempted several spells that all failed to destroy the barrier.

"It's incredible," admitted Gerald. "The tiniest of the Galdrs we've thrown against this wall would be enough to break open all the doors of Gifdu!"

"The Shadow's power is phenomenal," whispered Quadehar. "I've never come across a spell like this before!"

"I think," said Qadwan in a weary voice, "that it must have taken a long time to build this wall, even for The Shadow. It must already have been in position and he simply activated it when we arrived."

The elderly sorcerer was leaning against the door, still exhausted from the effort of climbing the stairs to the top of the tower. His theory explained why their efforts kept failing. A powerful spell that had been patiently woven could not easily be broken.

"Suppose we tried to conjure up the Insigil of the Lindorm?" suggested Gerald.

"The Dragon spell?" exclaimed Qadwan. "Are you crazy? We aren't even sure that it would be able to break the wall. And if the dragon escapes, we'll be in real trouble!"

"Qadwan's right," agreed Quadehar. "The Lindorm is potent but dangerous, and it would take as much energy to control it as to create it. We'll have to think of something else."

"Do you think the wall is as resistant on the inside as it is on the outside?" asked Kushumai abruptly.

"It's unlikely," stated Quadehar. "A wall like that is always built to withstand an attack from the outside. But that doesn't get us anywhere — we're still on the outside of it!"

"I have an idea," murmured the Huntress.

She went over to the invisible barrier and signaled to Amber.

34

THE TWIN SISTERS

"Amber? Come over here. . . ."

Amber hesitated, then went over to Kushumai.

"Who are you? I recognize your face. You appear to me in my dreams."

"No, you're wide awake, and this is no dream. I promise you I'll answer all your questions soon, but now is not the time! Do you want to help me save your friend?"

She pointed at Robin on the table.

Amber turned around: Robin was trembling from head to toe and quaking at each word The Shadow uttered. Tears came into her eyes again as she imagined what he must be going through.

"The High Priest of Bohor is drawing from him the strength he needs to destroy the resistance of the book of spells," Kushumai went on calmly.

"And . . . and then what?" Amber asked in a quavering voice.

"Your friend will die. You are the only person who can help him. . . ."

"But how? Please tell me!"

"By letting me do what I need to do. By giving yourself to me, little Hamingja. But I warn you, it will be painful."

"That doesn't matter," said Amber, fighting back her tears. "I'm prepared to do anything to save Robin's life."

"I knew it. You are brave, I know. I've always known. . . ."

The sorceress closed her eyes and began to hum a tune full of Graphems. On the other side of the barrier, Amber gave a raucous cry and flung back her head. Her eyes swiveled in their sockets, revealing the whites. A dull groan escaped her mouth. She slapped the palms of her hands heavily against the wall of energy. Her fingernails clawed the surface time and time again, faster and faster.

Huge beads of sweat ran down her face. She was still groaning, and the noise she made became more and more inhuman by the second. Suddenly she began to strike the barrier with the sides of her hands. As she did so, the wall began to crack.

"It's the first time I've seen anything like this!" exclaimed Gerald.

"There's something I don't understand," confessed Qadwan, who was feeling more lively. "Visibly, Kushumai has bewitched this girl and turned her into a Hamingja, a creature subject to her will. But to do that they had to have met before!"

"I'm not altogether surprised," interrupted Quadehar pensively. "Didn't you see the look on Amber's face when she saw Kushumai? I had the feeling they'd met before. Amber came back

from her last trip to The Uncertain World with terrible head-
aches. I thought it was the journey, but . . ."

". . . but it's the most common symptom of bewitchment,"
went on Qadwan.

"Yes, and I remember that there were a lot of holes in Amber's
account of her last visit to The Uncertain World, as if she had
forgotten," added Quadehar.

"Memory loss is also typical in these cases," concluded the
elderly sorcerer.

Cracks were beginning to appear around Amber's hands, which
were now glued to the energy wall. Kushumai, her eyes still shut
tight, was gasping as she chanted the magic words that kept her
in contact with Amber. Suddenly, Amber swayed and fell to
her knees, her hands still on the wall. She was trembling and
clearly exhausted.

"No," groaned Kushumai. "No! Keep going! We've nearly
done it!"

Coral watched her sister collapse against the invisible wall.
Without thinking, she rushed over to her and held her to support her.

"Amber? Are you all right? What has she done to you?"

But Amber was unable to reply. She was shivering violently as
if suffering from a raging fever. Coral was about to grab her
shoulders and lay her down on the floor when she felt a burning
sensation. She opened her mouth and cried out as much in surprise as with the pain. Just then, Amber seemed to recover. The
wall began to crack again around her hands.

"What's happening?" asked Gerald in amazement from the
other side of the magic wall.

"An extremely rare phenomenon, if I'm not mistaken," replied Quadehar. "Without being aware of it, Coral is transmitting her strength to her twin sister who's on the brink of exhaustion."

"Isn't that dangerous?" asked Qadwan nervously.

"Yes," said Quadehar curtly. "But Amber would probably be dying right now if Coral hadn't come to help her. . . ."

Coral did indeed feel her strength ebbing out of her body and into her sister's. At the same time, she realized that Amber was trembling less. She came to the conclusion that she was helping her, and that made it easier for her to bear the terrible pain in her face and all over her body. Instinctively, she looked at her forearm. Her soft, prettily tanned skin had become swollen and covered with sores and hideous scabs.

Panic-stricken, she raised a hand to her face, her pretty doll-like face that had broken so many boys' hearts. It felt rough to the touch. Her fingers were raw and bleeding. She screamed. It wasn't possible! This had to stop before she became completely disfigured.

She moved away from her sister and at once the pain abated. But Amber began to shiver all the more and the animal cry that came out of her mouth sounded as plaintive as that of a wounded beast.

Coral begin to cry softly. Was Amber going to die? She went over to her and once again flung her arms around her sister, hugging her as hard as she could, pouring all her love and affection into that embrace. What did her looks matter if Amber were no longer there to see her?

Quadehar, Gerald, and Qadwan had lumps in their throats. They stood there silent and solemn. The silence was only broken by the sound of The Shadow's incantations as he concentrated on his terrifying ritual, calling on Robin's powers to open the book of spells, and Kushumai's wailing as she drew on Amber's strength to smash the wall of energy.

Suddenly, with the sound of shattering glass, an entire section of the magic wall disintegrated, creating a doorway into the laboratory. Amber, Coral, and Kushumai all collapsed onto the floor, exhausted and unconscious. Quadehar and Gerald rushed forward.

"No! You stay and take care of them, Gerald!" said Quadehar.

The Shadow gave a howl of wrath. It was much too soon! Their ritual had not been completed. He had seen them attack the magic barrier but had thought it strong enough to withstand their most powerful sorcery. They were ruining everything. . . . Curse them!

The Shadow picked up the *Book of the Stars* in one hand and dragged Robin from the table with the other. He looked as if he were about to make his getaway.

"Stop!" ordered Quadehar. "Whoever you are, man, woman, or devil, I command you to hand over the boy and the book of spells!"

"Oh really," snickered The Shadow. "You think you can defeat me, you miserable sorcerer?"

With a cry of rage, Quadehar projected a Thursaz of The Uncertain World at him. The Shadow stopped the Graphem and it vanished into a fold in his vast cloak of shadows as easily as if it had been a little pebble. Quadehar quickly went on to weave a hasty Lokk based on the freezing Graphem, Ingwaz, but his spell met the same fate. Behind him, Gerald and Qadwan exchanged a rapid glance.

"Quick!" shouted Gerald, unwillingly abandoning the unconscious girls. "We've got to help Quadehar! We have to invoke the Insigil of the Lindorm. We have no choice. Ready?"

"I'm ready," said Qadwan, mustering all his remaining strength.

35

THE DRAGON SPELL

Never in his life had Quadehar faced such a powerful adversary. Not only were the spells he cast over The Shadow completely ineffective, but he also had to use all his knowledge to counter those The Shadow used against him.

The Shadow, however, was hindered by having to support Robin.

Seeing the young sorcerer partially concealed under the cloak of shadows and at the mercy of his terrible enemy strengthened Quadehar's resolve even further. He would never give up! He would not abandon his apprentice again.

"Let the boy go!" he shouted. "This is our struggle!"

The Shadow cackled and chanted a formula that made Quadehar's spirit quail.

Meanwhile, Qadwan and Gerald were preparing the formidable spell of the Insigil of the Lindorm.

When they had both mentally worked through the complex

enchantment, they exchanged a look. Then they took each other's hands and invoked the power of the Dragon:

"*Laukaz, Isaz, Naudhiz, Dagaz, Odala, Raidhu, Mannaz, Sea and Ice and Hand, Daylight, Possessed Lands, Chariot of the Sun illuminating the Ancestor, Talisman, Thurses, Skadi, Knights, Eagles, Nerthus, and Mani, create, awaken and guide, protect the spirits, deliver the undeliverable, let the spiral energy connect with the Powers! Vanish and give way to the Dragon of the Earth, for whom we embrace the Being of the Shadows! LINDORM!*"

At first, nothing happened. Then, with pounding hearts, the waiting sorcerers felt the earth shudder. With a great rumble, the dust rose and began to swirl faster and faster until it formed a winged serpent, which quickly grew to an enormous size. As soon as it was fully formed, it lit up from the inside with an unearthly glow. A huge mouth appeared at one end, beneath two chilling eyes as cold as ice. The combatants froze. The ghostly creature let out a wail, and its cry struck terror into the hearts of the entire kingdom. The Shadow himself staggered back. The dragon hesitated. It turned its infernal gaze on the two sorcerers who had dared conjure it up, and who themselves stood rigid with fear. It looked furious. Then, abruptly, it made for a fanlight and vanished through it into the world outside.

≈ ✳ ≈ ✳ ≈

The battle was still raging at the city gates. The arrival of the Warriors of the Steppes had restored the balance between the two sides that had been threatened a moment earlier by the sudden appearance of the bloodthirsty Commander Thunku accompanied by some fifty of the strongest and best-trained Orks. The men of the West and the bandits had suffered heavy losses in the combat and there were few of them left on the field. They preferred to take care of their wounded and leave the fighting to their allies whose profession was war.

The Purple Forest contingent, all seasoned huntsmen, were putting up a good fight. The knights were living up to their reputation as exceptional fighters and the monsters attacking them were taking a harsh beating. The Warriors of the Steppes engaged Thunku's elite Orks, and at last found opponents of their own caliber. Meanwhile, the Men of the Sands continued to snipe at the priests from nearby houses, while the Korrigans had fun and games countering the spells being cast by the priests on the ramparts.

But two men in particular stood out, dominating the battle and bringing murmurs of admiration to the lips of all the fighters.

Like a war god with his huge sword and his bloodstained armor of metal and leather, Tofann thrust and parried, lunged and smashed, blocked and battered amid howls of rage and pain from the Orks.

Nearby, Urian Penmarch, like a wild Titan with his battered turquoise armor and giant axe glinting in the sunlight, was cutting down his opponents with the ease of a woodcutter felling trees. Foaming at the mouth, his eyes blazing and his gray beard dripping with sweat, the veteran knight was paying a final tribute to Valentino.

A groaning Ork suddenly pointed in amazement to the top of the Tower in the center of Yenibohor. Moments later, they all saw a huge serpent of light rise up into the sky, stop dead, and let out a howl of pain, then descend again swiftly to disappear through a window.

≈ ✳ ≈ ✳ ≈

The dragon only vanished for a few seconds. When it came back into the room it had just left, it froze, writhed, opened its jaws wide, and howled again. Then it leaped at The Shadow and went straight through him.

The Shadow cried out and crumpled, letting Robin and the book of spells drop to the floor. But he staggered to his feet again: He was still alive!

The dragon seemed surprised. It darted its icy gaze at the strange figure who should have dropped dead. The dragon had been created to take a life, and had failed to do so. It turned its head toward the sorcerers who had invoked it, looked at the old man, and saw fear in his eyes. He'd do instead. Outside, where it had tried to escape from its new masters, the dragon had been wounded by the daylight. The void was more restful. To get back there, it had to accomplish its mission one way or another. The beast struck like lightning and vanished instantly amid a shower of golden sparks.

"Qadwan!" yelled Gerald.

The sorcerer could only stand by helplessly while the Earth Dragon attacked his old friend. Quadehar got there before him: He rushed forward and caught Qadwan in his arms. The old sorcerer had died instantaneously; he hadn't suffered. The dragon had taken his spirit with him. There was a serene smile on his face. Quadehar gently laid his body on the cold flagstones and all eyes converged on The Shadow.

He had survived the attack of the Insigil of the Lindorm. It was unbelievable. As far back as any of the sorcerers could remember, this was the first time that someone had escaped from the Dragon! But The Shadow had not emerged unscathed; his powers had been considerably weakened. He was still unsteady on his feet and the cloak of darkness concealing him was in tatters. The Shadow's disguise disintegrated as scraps fell to the floor with a crackling sound, and fizzled away.

When The Shadow's true face was revealed, the sorcerers cried out in shock.

For there stood an old man shrouded in the dark cloak of the Guild whose face they knew well. But this man was no longer either weak or stooped. And he returned the gaze of the astounded sorcerers with the eyes of someone who had never been blind. His cold laughter, uninterrupted by any coughing fits, jolted them out of their dazed stupor.

"Charfalaq!"

The Shadow was indeed the Chief Sorcerer of Gifdu.

36
THE TRUTH BEHIND THE
CLOAK OF SHADOWS

Lord Sha had at last finished off the priests who had come running to provide backup. Not one of them had managed to get through the door of the Tower. He had fought them relentlessly, spells versus evil enchantments, Graphems versus sinister formulas. And he had defeated them, one after another.

Breathless, exhausted by his efforts, he made his way up the staircase and appeared in The Shadow's laboratory.

He was greeted by the sight of the motionless bodies of Kushumai and the two girls lying on the floor. Then he caught sight of the lifeless body of Qadwan, then Gerald and Quadehar who stood facing a familiar-looking old man.

"The Shadow? Surely . . . it can't be?" said Yorwan to himself in amazement as he went over to join his sorcerer friends.

Gerald spoke to Charfalaq, with tears in his eyes:

"But why, Master . . . ? Why?"

The old man looked the computer expert up and down disdainfully.

"Above all, so as not to be like you, with no other ambition than to tinker with computers!"

Gerald went purple in the face with anger, but said nothing more. Charfalaq was trying to upset them, to paralyze them by making them angry. They knew they must not rise to the bait.

The Chief Sorcerer then turned to Lord Sha.

"Well, well! Yorwan, the brilliant and promising young sorcerer who left Gifdu rather hurriedly. You missed the battle by the look of things. Desertion's your speciality, isn't it? Tell me, now that we have no secrets from each other, what made you run off with the *Book of the Stars*?"

"A cry for help that came from the Book itself," replied Yorwan who, seizing the opportunity to explain his behavior once and for all to his companions, did not allow Charfalaq's unpleasant insinuations to rile him. "I suppose you tried to decipher the forbidden pages. Well, you unwittingly set off a magic alarm that alerted the Bear Society of the danger. I had not long been appointed The Lost Isle's representative of this very ancient society. It was my job to remove the book of spells to a safe place. It was a vague threat; the Book wasn't very specific. So as not to take any risks, I chose to go into exile in the remotest corner of The Uncertain World. . . ."

"How terribly touching!" snickered Charfalaq. "And there was me thinking that, like that idiot Urian, you had run away to get out of marrying that silly Alicia!"

Gerald placed a hand on Yorwan's shoulder to calm him down. They absolutely must not allow themselves to be provoked by this vicious old man.

The Chief Sorcerer tried his luck with Quadehar:

"And you, Quadehar, the greatest sorcerer the Guild has ever produced! So sincere, so upright, so honest! That must have been painful, being called a traitor!"

"So you were behind that nasty business," grumbled Quadehar. "You planned the ambush at Jaghatel with Thunku! You appointed me to lead the expedition so that I could be blamed for its failure if I escaped alive. Curse you! You sent all the sorcerers who came with me to certain death."

"I admit my plan was well thought out. There were only two things missing: the *Book of the Stars*, which Lord Sha had stolen from me and which he never allowed out of his sight, and Robin, the famous boy with astonishing powers. He was mentioned in the Book and I sought him for so long in The Uncertain World where it was written that he was to be found, when in fact he was in The Lost Isle, right under my nose. In sending you, Quadehar, into a trap along with the Guild's best sorcerers, I isolated Robin. I sent Lord Sha an anonymous letter informing him that a boy who might be his son was alone at Gifdu, so as to lure him away from the book of spells. Thus I was able to recover the first missing element. As for the second, he certainly led me a song and dance, but I managed to lay my hands on him in the end!"

Talking all the while, Charfalaq had drawn closer to the Book and to Robin. Too engrossed by what he was saying, the sorcerers hadn't realized what he was doing.

"But why?" repeated Gerald, who found it hard to accept the appalling truth. "Why? Weren't you content to be Master of the Guild, one of the most influential and respected men on The Lost Isle?"

"You're wrong, Gerald: I am the *only* powerful figure on The Lost Isle!" boasted Charfalaq. "And thanks to The Shadow's reputation, I kept the population in a state of fear, allowing the Guild to obtain more and more privileges at the expense of the Brotherhood of the Knights. I am also the true Master of The Uncertain World over which I rule, thanks to my priests, by striking terror into people's hearts."

"You'll pay for that, too!" threatened Quadehar, marching toward him.

Suddenly, Charfalaq grabbed the Book and picked up Robin from the floor with a speed and energy that belied his years.

"If you come near me, I'll kill him!" he warned calmly.

Quadehar stopped dead.

"That's better," said the Chief Sorcerer. "I do, in fact, need the boy to open the last pages of the Book and reveal the spells that will help me to transport the Graphems to The Real World. When that is done, magic will reign over the entire multiverse, and nothing will be able to prevent me from extending my powers infinitely and becoming the absolute Master of the three Worlds!"

"I will stop you!" threatened Quadehar again, clenching his fists.

"Oh no, you'll do nothing of the sort! You wouldn't like me to hurt your son now, would you?"

There was a gasp of astonishment in the laboratory. Nobody could believe what they had just heard.

"Oh?" said the old man with mock innocence. "You didn't know! Or you didn't want to know. . . . Tut, tut! You never had the curiosity to go and see inside his mind? I don't blame you. I myself had to wait for the Graphems to go to sleep before I could rummage inside his skull. But all the same, fathers aren't what they used to be! Starting with you, Yorwan, who's prepared to risk his life for a book of spells, but whose own son was abandoned in the desert sands. . . ."

"You're lying!" cried Quadehar.

"What do you mean, you spiteful old man?" asked Yorwan.

"Ask the Huntress!"

By keeping the conversation going and capturing the sorcerers' interest, Charfalaq had managed to edge toward a large flagstone that was different from the others. It was covered with deeply etched signs. Quadehar suddenly realized the danger. He leaped forward, but too late. Charfalaq uttered a few words and disappeared instantly, taking Robin and the *Book of the Stars* with him.

"A vanishing spell!" groaned Gerald, as it dawned on him what the Chief Sorcerer had been up to.

"They could be anywhere. It's going to be very difficult to locate them," sighed Quadehar, distraught.

A profound silence filled with despair and resignation fell over the room. It was all over, and they knew it: They had played, and they had lost.

Just then, puffing and panting, Romaric, Godfrey, Bertram, and Kyle burst into the laboratory.

"What's happened?" asked Bertram.

"Robin! Where's Robin?" cried Romaric.

The grief-stricken sorcerers didn't need to say a word: A glance around the room was enough for the youngsters to grasp the scale of the disaster.

37

THE TEMPLE

The Chief Sorcerer, Robin, and the *Book of the Stars* reappeared in a room that was much bigger than the one they had just left. The yellowing walls were hung with embroidered tapestries depicting scenes from the life of the evil Bohor. Oil lamps on stands gave out an orange glow and a number of ritual objects lay on a small round table in one corner. The vanishing spell had whisked them to a temple of Bohor, in Yadigar, to be exact.

Charfalaq was delighted that he'd had the brainwave of engraving the spell on a flagstone in his laboratory. A smile of satisfaction hovered on his lips. He was particularly pleased at the way he'd used the faithful Lomgo in various guises to infiltrate the seats of power in The Uncertain World: adviser to Commander Thunku, Lord Sha's butler . . . that was how he had finally managed to steal the precious book of spells from Jaghatel. And although Thunku's successive attempts to kidnap Robin from The Lost Isle had all failed, it was still thanks to Thunku that he was now safely hidden away in the city of Yadigar. The Chief Sorcerer frowned briefly: Where had Lomgo gotten to? He hadn't seen him since those idiots had dared to attack Yenibohor. He shrugged. Now nothing mattered any longer, other than the Book and this boy who would give him access to the secret spells within it. Soon, he would be Master of the three Worlds!

He paused to give Robin a few sips of the elixir of life, then led him outside.

The city was deserted. Only a few groups of drunken rough-neck soldiers were roaming the streets. Thunku's entire army of Orks was in Yenibohor and so were the priests who usually served at the temple. The Chief Sorcerer took the external stair-case that went up to the top of the pyramid-shaped temple.

Robin was invigorated by the sorcerer's potion. After the epi-sode with the horrible tortoise, he had been disconnected from his surroundings and it had taken him some time to emerge, first of all on the cold floor of his cell, and then on the hard tabletop in the laboratory. The memory of the tortoise filled him with ter-ror. In comparison, The Shadow was almost a delightful companion! The Shadow . . . or rather the Chief Sorcerer — he had never liked the old man who had scared him the very first time they had met on The Lost Isle, in the Provost's Palace. This impression had been reinforced after he'd overheard his conver-sation with Master Quadehar, a conversation that had driven him to run away from Gifdu. . . . What a liar, what a hypocrite! This man, who was respected, if not loved, by everybody, had hoodwinked them all, limping and coughing and spluttering like an invalid, pretending to be half-blind and half-senile, making everyone feel sorry for him. He would pretend to be resting in his apartments at the monastery and then slip off to The Uncertain World to terrorize and persecute people as The Shadow.

Robin glared vindictively at the perfectly robust old man climbing the stairs and dragging him along behind. He would have tried to run away, but he knew from the way his legs were trembling that he wouldn't get far. He decided to preserve the precious little strength the potion had given him to try and stand up to the sorcerer when he began his ritual to open the *Book of the Stars* again.

They reached the flattened tip of the temple that overlooked part of the city. In the distance, Robin could see the Stone Road and the Ravenous Desert beyond, where his friend Kyle lived.

"Robin, since you're conscious now and we have more time for niceties," said Charfalaq in an almost cheerful voice, "I'm asking you one last time. Will you, of your own free will, help me break the spells protecting this book, or must I again enlist your aid by force?"

"You're right, I'm conscious again," replied Robin, thrusting out his chin defiantly. "You just try forcing me to do anything! I will resist you with every ounce of my strength!"

"Tut, tut," sneered the Chief Sorcerer. "A young cockerel, that's what you are! A young cockerel trying to cover up his physical weakness by crowing noisily. And tell me, just what can the young cockerel do against this old fox?"

He raised his arm and composed a series of Mudra — gestures which invoke the Graphems by reproducing their forms. Overcome by the Chief Sorcerer's magic, Robin collapsed. In vain he tried to call up the Graphems to break the spell that had paralyzed him and kept him mercilessly pinned to the ground. But either they were still sleeping inside him after The Shadow's last sinister attack, or he had overestimated his strength: He lay there completely helpless.

"Master! Master Quadehar! Please!" he began to pray inwardly. "Don't leave me like this! I don't want to be Charfalaq's instrument of evil! Please don't leave me alone!"

In his mind, behind his tear-filled eyes, the image of his Master appeared. It was the image he loved best, where Quadehar was smiling at him affectionately before clasping him in a protective embrace. He pictured himself resting his head on his shoulder, closing his eyes, no longer thinking of anything. His Master had one hand on Robin's head and he kept saying that he was a good apprentice, sensible. And clever . . .

A rush of adrenalin made Robin snap out of his desperate daydream. Clever, intelligent . . . He'd just had a brainwave. A brilliant idea! There was a million to one chance that it would work. But it was the only, the last, the very last chance! It was a crazy idea. Delightfully, terrifyingly crazy! But to carry it out, he had to regain some freedom of movement.

"You win!" he blurted out, as if he had given up the fight. "I can't go on anymore! I agree to help you. Just stop the pain."

Charfalaq stared at him in amazement. The boy was giving in now, after having resisted him for days on end? What did that mean? He gave him a wary look. Was this some new trick? But there in front of him Robin was truly distraught and the tears running down his face were genuine. After all, the boy knew he was lost, he was desperate. He was a long way away from his friends and could no longer cling to the hope that they would come and save him. It made sense for him to give up. Once hope has died, it is impossible to go on suffering! Charfalaq's face broke into a triumphant smile. If the boy agreed to cooperate, things would be a lot easier. With a sweeping gesture, he released Robin from the spell pinning him to the ground.

≋ ✳ ≋ ✳ ≋

In Yenibohor, the battle was drawing to a close. The Orks, demoralized at the sight of the priests being shot down one by one by the Men of the Sands, and disheartened by the relentless zeal of the knights and the Warriors of the Steppes, were surrendering by the dozen. They were disarmed and taken to the city's prison. Now it was their turn to be held captive after having sent so many unfortunates to the cells. The few priests still alive also gave themselves up and, with looks of bitter resentment, allowed themselves to be chained up without a word.

"They must be wondering why Bohor, their all-powerful demon, hasn't come to their rescue!" jeered the instrument maker who had led the farmers of the West into battle.

"They'll find out soon enough that their Bohor was nothing but the invention of a man, a man who concealed himself beneath the appearance of a demon, to commit acts that even a demon wouldn't have dared," replied Kushumai weakly.

The Huntress had come out of the tower, supported by two hunters.

"I can't understand how the priests managed to inspire such fear!"

"People's hearts and minds are filled with fear," said the Huntress. "It is enough to give a face to those fears."

Tofann and the Commander arrived, still breathless from the fighting.

"That's it, Kushumai," declared the warrior. "The last pockets of resistance are gradually surrendering. We are in full control of the city."

"Excellent!" replied Kushumai, overjoyed. "Have you tracked down Thunku? I think some of us would like to say few a words to him!"

The Commander stiffened.

"I'm afraid there's no trace of Thunku for the time being. Nothing."

"Huh . . . he'll crawl out of the woodwork eventually, when we search Yenibohor with a fine-toothed comb."

Tofann jerked his head in the direction of the Tower.

"How did things go up there?"

"Badly," replied Kushumai. "The Shadow managed to escape with Robin and the book of spells. The youngsters who were in the tower are fine. Right now, Quadehar, Yorwan, and Gerald are trying to break the spell that The Shadow used to escape. But there's more — the elderly sorcerer Qadwan was killed during the confrontation."

"The archer who led the bandits is also badly wounded," stated the Commander, bowing his head.

"We will pay tribute to them when all this is over," said Tofann, clenching his fists.

"I only hope that this end you speak of will not also be the end of all the people we love," replied Kushumai gloomily.

38

THE POEM OF WISDOM

The Chief Sorcerer opened the *Book of the Stars,* which he'd been holding under his arm, and Robin, drawing near, was at last able to get a close look at it. It was a big book, the size of a school register, but thicker. It had a shabby, soft leather cover worn thin over the years by generations of hands. The book of spells was studded with myriad stars, which made it look almost alive. Inside, the yellowing pages were covered in lines and lines of signs and symbols laboriously inscribed in midnight-blue ink.

When Charfalaq was two-thirds of the way through the hefty tome, he stopped. The last part of the book was utterly beyond his grasp. It was meant to be.

"Since you have agreed to be my assistant for the opening ritual, you must follow my instructions to the letter."

"So I'm your assistant just for the ritual?" asked Robin, pretending to be disappointed and looking displeased. "I seem to remember you offering me a proper partnership, and even to share your power with me. That's what you promised."

"Yes, yes, all right," said Charfalaq irritably. "Very well, you will be prime minister of my future empire!" he continued, sounding utterly insincere. "But first of all, we have to make the book reveal all its secrets. Prepare yourself. . . ."

Robin acted as if he were happy with the Chief Sorcerer's ridiculous promise and listened carefully to his instructions. It turned out to be quite straightforward: He just had to hold the Book and concentrate very hard, and repeat the magic words that Charfalaq was going to recite.

The apprentice placed his hands on the *Book of the Stars*. At once he felt a delicious tingling sensation and the Graphems dormant deep down inside him began to stir and hum.

"Good! I can see from the color coming back into your cheeks that the book of spells is happy to be in your hands. And a good thing, too!"

Charfalaq began his incantation. It was very long. Luckily, he stopped frequently to allow Robin to repeat what he had just said.

Robin did his best. He tried all the harder as the Graphems seemed to be taking a curious delight in the strange ritual. Soon they were all there: Fehu, Uruz, Thursaz, Ansuz, Raidhu, Kenaz, Gebu, Wunjo, Hagal, Naudhiz, Isaz, Yera, Eihwaz, Perthro, Elhaz, Sowelo, Teiwaz, Berkana, Ehwo, Mannaz, Laukaz, Ingwaz, Dagaz, and Odala. The twenty-four Graphems of the alphabet of the stars were all there, in his stomach, his chest, and his head, glowing and quivering as never before. Graphems that the teachings of Master Quadehar had sown deep down inside him, that had taken root and grown in the richest and most powerful Ond that any human being had ever possessed. Graphems which, nourished by such a force, had almost become living entities in their own right, independent and capable of substituting their will for that of their host when necessary. And now they were all there, standing to attention in the presence of the Book that had invented them, that had created them.

Charfalaq was sweating profusely with the effort required to carry out the ritual. The Graphems continued to grow in strength, fascinated by the presence of the book of spells. Robin mechanically repeated the sorcerer's magic words while at the same time reciting in his head the ancient poem of wisdom for apprentice sorcerers which his master was so fond of:

Know how to write and to interpret,
Feel the colors and the shapes
When to cast and when to cast off,
Then know your Graphem's measured fate.
Sometimes it's better not to ask the question
When the answer's in the Stars.
Feel the strength as it grows within you
And find your gift will reap its own reward.

His master was forever telling him that one day he would understand the meaning of these words. Well, that day had come! He couldn't explain why, but the more he thought about those lines in which he had found a number of solutions to his problems, the more convinced he was that they meant a lot more than anybody believed. This poem was in the first chapter of the *Book of the Stars*, right after the section entitled "The Words of the Crier," a fundamental text that told how the book of spells had originated. There must have been a reason for that: The Book began by giving a key to anybody who wanted to take it, and a key can be used to close as well as to open a door. . . .

At one point in the incantation, the book of spells gave out an alarm, as it had done before to alert the Bear Society that it was in danger, and the Graphems became agitated. Robin could feel the turmoil inside him. He tried to reassure them by asking them to trust him. The Graphems calmed down.

Suddenly, Charfalaq started chanting faster and louder. Robin guessed that the ritual was coming to a climax. Which meant that it would soon have succeeded. . . . Robin closed his eyes and joined in the sorcerer's excitement. Called up by an overpowering force, the Graphems inside Robin rose up again and froze. Robin used all his strength to prevent the sixteenth Graphem, Sowelo, from doing likewise. He desperately needed Sowelo for his plan to work!

"*Feel the strength as it grows within you*

And find your gift will reap its own reward," he said to himself, to boost his courage.

When he sensed that the incantation was at its height, when he felt the Book tremble in his hands, when the Graphems became incandescent behind his eyelids, he silently invoked Sowelo, the Graphem of power and of the sun, of terrifying fire and devastating victories.

"*By the power of the Wheel and the Root, great source of nourishment, powerful energy that smashes barriers, I bow before the sacred and appeal to your goodwill! Free us and send each to his destiny! SOWELO!"*

The Graphem hummed, began to quiver, and then exploded. Robin screamed. The Chief Sorcerer stopped in mid-sentence. Round-eyed with disbelief, he saw Robin light up from the inside and ignite, consumed by cold flames. A column of light burst from the screaming boy and shot up into the sky. Then the fire spread to the *Book of the Stars*, and Charfalaq gasped. A second column of energy leaped from the pages of the book of spells.

"NOOO!"

But the Chief Sorcerer didn't have time to move a muscle: The flames leaped from the Book to him. He groaned, and his groan turned into a howl of pain, and then despair, and finally of agony when a third column of light appeared and joined the other two, rising up toward the stars.

When the incredible mass of magic energy finally stopped shooting up into space, Robin slid gently to the ground. He looked as if he had lost consciousness again, but his breathing was regular and his expression peaceful: He was asleep.

The *Book of the Stars* also fell onto the ground and the gathering evening breeze ruffled its pages. From about two-thirds of the way through, the pages were blank, completely blank, as if they had never been written on.

Beside the Book, on the spot where Charfalaq had stood a few moments earlier, there was a heap of dust that gradually dispersed in the wind. Quadehar had been right to say to his pupil one day that magic fed less off some bodies than some bodies fed off magic! Once the Graphems had gone, the Chief Sorcerer of the Guild and High Priest of Bohor had crumpled, disintegrated, and vanished.

And lastly, among the stars gradually appearing in the heavens, two new constellations began to shine, born from the magic that had risen up to the skies.

39

AFTER THE BATTLE

Night had fallen over Yenibohor. The moans of the wounded rose from the makeshift camps set up by the army of the Hills in the vanquished city. Men searched the houses in the hope of finding tables, chairs, and even mattresses to make their night more comfortable after the rigors of the battlefield. The huge prison was crammed with the priests who had escaped the Men of the Sands' bullets, and the surviving Orks from Thunku's army. The dead were laid out in rows in the avenue facing the city gates. There were a few outbursts of laughter from around the fires that were being lit one by one, but above all there was an atmosphere of profound weariness.

On discovering Amber and Coral lying unconscious on the floor of the laboratory, Romaric, Godfrey, Bertram, and Kyle had immediately rushed to their rescue. Eventually, the girls had come around and Gerald went over to say some comforting words to them, leaving Quadehar and Lord Sha to do their utmost to break The Shadow's vanishing spell. As soon as the twins were able to stand, the sorcerer accompanied all six of them down to the base of the Tower. On the way, they badgered him to tell them everything that had happened, in detail. Then he handed the friends over to a knight who guided them to a house near the tower.

There they found Thomas lying on a straw mattress and being tended to by Agatha and Toti. Amber, still very weak, leaned on Bertram, who would not have entrusted her to anybody else. Coral, whose face and skin had gone back to normal — to her great relief — was supported by Romaric. Two knights answering to the names of Ambor and Bertolen, exhaustion written all over their faces and their armor badly damaged from the fighting, had been given specific orders by the Commander and Kushumai to stay with them and to be both vigilant and kind.

"How are you doing, Thomas?" asked Godfrey gently, going over to the wounded boy.

"My shoulder and leg are killing me," replied Thomas gruffly. "But apparently if I can still feel them, it's a good sign!"

"It's an even better sign that you're still able to joke about it," said Agatha through gritted teeth. She seemed tired of having to play the nurse, which she had reluctantly agreed to do.

"Thank you for staying with him, Agatha," said Godfrey, placing a hand on her arm.

"Toti's the one you should thank, not me. He's the one who took care of Thomas."

While talking, Agatha let her hand casually fall onto Godfrey's, and he kept it there.

"Oh, it's nothing," said Toti awkwardly.

"Come here, Toti," said Kyle. "I'm proud of you," he went

on, hugging him a little awkwardly because he was a boy of the Desert and a boy of the Desert wasn't allowed to show his feelings. "You're a credit to The Uncertain World!"

Ambor and Bertolen remained at a discreet distance so as not to get in the way of the children who had all, in their own way, acted like true heroes in this battle.

"What about . . . Robin?" Agatha ventured.

"Gone. Snatched by The Shadow. The sorcerers couldn't stop him. They're on their trail . . . ," replied Amber, whose chin was wobbling as if she were going to start crying.

"Come on, Amber, you know we all did everything we possibly could," Coral consoled her. "Especially you."

"It's not true." She hiccupped. "I was bewitched by that woman with green eyes. I obeyed her will. But you, Coral, nobody forced you to come and help me! You were in a lot of pain, I could feel it, but you stuck by me, and you saved my life!"

She burst into tears on her sister's shoulder and hugged her tight. Coral stroked her hair and began to cry, too. Nobody dared say a word. It was the first time Amber's friends had seen her cry. Even if they hadn't witnessed the scene in the Tower, they knew that Coral had shown a courage that they doubted they would have been capable of themselves.

Urian Penmarch suddenly burst into the room. He was tousled and his face was still smeared with blood. He gave off a powerful smell of sweat. Ambor and Bertolen rose and greeted him respectfully. The old knight had fought like a lion. . . . Urian went over to the young people. He patted his nephew Romaric's cheek affectionately, then boomed:

"Which of you is Toti?"

"I am," replied the boy shyly.

"Do you have a brother known as the archer, who was in charge of the bandits' brigade?"

"Yes. Wh . . . why?"

Urian looked him straight in the eye and said gently,

"Be brave, my boy. Your brother is dead. Killed in battle. On the field of honor."

Toti bowed his head. Tears welled up in his eyes. He followed Urian out of the house, walking mechanically like a robot. His friends all filed out, too, except Thomas of course, who said he didn't mind being left alone.

The archer's body had been placed outside the house by a dozen bandits, by torchlight. When Toti appeared on the threshold, they all stepped forward ceremoniously and gravely shook his hand. Toti stood there, motionless, for a long time. Then he flung himself on to his brother's body and poured out his grief, crying and punching the archer's lifeless chest.

"You've left! You've abandoned me. . . . Now I'm all alone!"

"Stop that, son," said Urian, raising him to his feet. "Your brother isn't coming back. You must show yourself to be worthy of his sacrifice."

Toti calmed down a little. He looked away from his brother's body, went up to Urian, and clasped his hand. The old knight looked a little taken aback.

"Poor Toti," murmured Romaric. "We should try and comfort him."

A commotion prevented the gang from going over to console the unhappy Toti. Three men had just come out of the Tower. One of them was carrying a young boy.

≈ ✳ ≈ ✳ ≈

Quadehar stepped out of the tower bearing Robin in his arms. He was followed by Yorwan and Gerald, who was hugging the big star-studded black book to his chest. A huge crowd surged forward to greet them. The men of the army of the Hills knew that the sorcerers had been playing out the last act of this daring war against The Shadow. . . . The sorcerers were greeted with shouts of joy and cheers, for the crowd guessed that if they were alive, it meant The Shadow had perished. Kushumai, who had found renewed strength and was now able to walk unsupported by her hunters, was among the first to acclaim them.

"You did it!" she said. "You overpowered the Chief Sorcerer and you've brought Robin back! That's wonderful!"

"We did nothing," Gerald corrected her. "We merely disabled the vanishing spell used by Charfalaq and borrowed it ourselves. We reappeared in the city of Yadigar, in a temple dedicated to the demon Bohor. We found Robin unconscious on the temple roof, lying next to the Book of the Stars and a heap of dust. No sign of the Chief Sorcerer. I have no idea what happened, but clearly Robin defeated him on his own."

The sorcerer's explanations left them all baffled.

"The main thing," exclaimed Kushumai, "is that the evil old sorcerer wasn't able to carry out his ritual! Our two Worlds, and even The Real World, which never even knew the danger it was in, have been saved!"

"How's Robin?" asked the Commander, coming over to them.

"He's very weak, but he's breathing normally," replied Quadehar.

"Robin!"

Barging their way through the throng gathered in front of The Shadow's tower, Robin's friends raced over to Quadehar.

At the sight of her unconscious friend, Amber gave a heart-rending scream:

"He's dead! Oh, he's dead! He's dead!"

"Calm down, Amber!" said Gerald. "He's alive. Robin's alive!"

Amber gave a huge sigh of relief. She rushed over to caress, with a trembling hand, the sleeping boy's cheek. Robin stirred, struggled to open his eyes, stared at something in front of him, and then closed them again.

"Are you sure he's all right?" asked Coral anxiously.

"Yes. He just needs rest. Lots of rest."

Amber seemed calmer. She gazed at Robin with a strange expression.

"It's weird," she said dreamily. "I'd forgotten how green his eyes are!"

Quadehar and Kushumai exchanged a glance.

"His mother's eyes," murmured Quadehar. "I think the two of us should have a little chat," he added, looking at the Huntress.

"The three of us," Yorwan corrected him.

He turned to Kyle. The boy looked up at him.

"So, is what Gerald told me true? Are you . . . Am I . . . ?"

"I am your father, Kyle," said Yorwan, "and your mother, Alicia, lives on The Lost Isle. She believes Robin is her son, but Kushumai switched you for Robin when you were a baby and entrusted you, if I'm not mistaken, to the kindness of the People of the Desert. . . ."

"It's true," said Kushumai in a quavering voice, remembering the heartache when she had had to leave her baby son, Robin, to someone else's care. . . .

At that precise moment, the Huntress was no longer the pitiless warrior, nor even the cold sorceress they all knew. For a split second, she appeared as she was deep down inside: A mother who had been forced to abandon her child for his own protection.

But Kushumai quickly regained her composure.

"All in good time. For the moment, it is essential that Quadehar take Robin back to The Lost Isle to receive medical treatment. And I need to talk to Amber. I owe her an apology."

Then she turned to Quadehar, with a strange smile.

"It's not party time yet, Quadehar, but it soon will be. And that will also be our moment. Be ready. . . ."

She turned to Amber, put a gentle arm around her shoulders, and led her to one side.

40

DAYDREAMS

Robin tossed and turned in bed, sighing. He'd been stuck in this hospital room in Dashtikazar for a whole month now. It was a very pleasant room, decorated in blue and white, which he had all to himself. One window looked out over the heath and the other over the sea, and there were fresh flowers everywhere, which the nurses, who couldn't do enough for him, changed every day; but it was beginning to feel like prison again.

When Quadehar, Yorwan, and Gerald had found him on the temple roof, he'd been so weak that at first the doctors had doubted whether he would even survive. Then, thanks to their treatment and care, he had gradually grown stronger, and now they were only keeping him in the hospital as a precaution. Luckily, he could rely on visits to fill his days. He received so many that the head doctor had had to step in and ask the Provost to draw up a list of authorized visitors.

"Mas — Dad!" exclaimed Robin, spotting Quadehar, who had tiptoed silently into the room.

"Hello, Son," replied the sorcerer with a broad grin. "So how's our hero today?"

The saga of the knights' expedition and the siege of Yenibohor by the army of the Hills was the sole topic of conversation on The Lost Isle. And Robin's combat against Charfalaq was already a legend. He had already earned a special place in the hearts of the population of The Lost Isle after rescuing Agatha from the clutches of the monsters of The Uncertain World. Now he was a national hero, and was becoming a living legend. From the minute he returned, groups of admirers thronged the hospital lobby wanting to thank him for having freed them from the threat of The Shadow. Their gratitude was very touching, but also exhausting. Especially as Robin desperately needed calm and solitude to mull over all the events that had turned his life upside down in such a short space of time.

"Don't call me a hero; it's not funny," said Robin, sitting up in bed.

"I'm not making fun of you," replied Quadehar, going over to Robin and stroking his cheek affectionately. "Quite the opposite, I'm very proud of you. And so is your mother, believe me. I mean, Alicia . . ."

The first shock, of course, had been to learn that his mother wasn't his real mother. Although Robin had suspected it, the truth was still hard.

It had been very painful for Alicia, too, who had sobbed and clasped him to her, refusing to let go, repeating that he would always be her son. He recalled gazing at her lovingly and saying that for him, nothing would change, that his life with her in Penmarch would go on as usual. Did he dream of his real mother? she had asked, devastated. His real mother . . .

So Robin's real mother was that woman with green eyes who had turned Amber into a terrible Hamingja. She lived among the wild beasts in a dark forest in The Uncertain World and also ruled over the men of a secret society. That wasn't quite his idea of a mother, Robin had told Alicia, and shyly admitted to Kushumai when she came to see him one day in hospital.

Kushumai had smiled at him and stroked his hair, and had replied that she was sorry things had turned out the way they had. That she regretted having had to abandon him. But because she had had to remove him from the world of the priests of Yenibohor and take responsibility for so many people, she could not allow herself to be ruled by her feelings. She was disappointed he wouldn't be coming with her, but understood his feelings for Alicia and accepted his decision to stay with her on The Lost Isle. She just hoped that he would come and visit her some-times. . . . Robin had replied that he most certainly would. He promised to visit her when he went to The Uncertain World with Alicia to see Kyle.

For Kyle was Alicia's real son, the boy Kushumai had stolen and left in the Ravenous Desert for the People of the Sands to find. He was the child Yorwan had fathered. The Shadow had been speaking the truth when he had told Yorwan this to lure him away from Jaghatel. What The Shadow hadn't known then was that Kyle was a changeling. That was why Lord Sha hadn't been able to identify Robin in his underground hideout at Gifdu.

And now Yorwan was reunited with Alicia, the love of his life, and the son he had been looking for. The only fly in the ointment was that Kyle obstinately refused to come and live on The Lost Isle. His home was in the Ravenous Desert, among the Men of the Sands. But Yorwan, who knew and respected the People of the Desert, had soon come to accept his decision, especially as traveling between the two worlds was now so easy. However, it was much harder for Alicia, who had cried for ages, but had finally been won over by Yorwan and Kyle's arguments. All the same, Kyle was thrilled to be reunited with his true parents, and they promised to get together often, in The Uncertain World for the solstices and on The Lost Isle for the equinoxes.

"I bet you're going to tell me that you just dropped in to give me a hug — which you haven't given me, by the way! And that you've got a lot of work, you can't stay . . ." said Robin.

"Don't be angry with me," Quadehar sighed. "Right now everyone wants me, as if I'd suddenly become indispensable! I promise you we'll make up for lost time later, when you're out of here. . . ."

"Don't worry, I don't mind," Robin reassured him, taking his hand. "I'm just teasing."

The second shock awaiting Robin had been the discovery that his father, the man he believed to be in permanent exile in The Real World and whom he had so desperately wanted to get to know, was . . . Master Quadehar! And Master Quadehar had been as astonished as he had been at the revelation! Kushumai had never told him she was expecting a child and as they had soon lost touch with each other, the sorcerer had had no means of knowing.

And lastly, the relationship between Quadehar and Robin had completely changed. Quadehar had always felt a bond between himself and Robin, and now the master-pupil relationship quickly turned into a father-son one. This change had been all the easier as Robin — and this was the third shock — could no longer remain an apprentice sorcerer.

He had lost all his magic powers. They had evaporated into the ether when he had called upon Sowelo to destroy The Shadow.

It had taken him a while to accept that no Graphem would ever answer his call again. Just like Lord Sha in The Real World, he felt merely ordinary.

"I've brought you something to read," said Quadehar, putting a few adventure books down on the bedside table. "But all these stories must seem a bit tame to you now!"

"Oh no! It's fun reading about extraordinary things that happen to others, especially from the comfort of my own bed."

"Get better quickly," said the sorcerer, taking leave of his erstwhile apprentice. "I can't wait till we can resume our walks on the heath!"

Robin gazed at him imploringly. Quadehar gave him an awkward smile, then suddenly made up his mind. He leaned over, kissed his son on the forehead, and embraced him. Robin was overjoyed.

"Be good!" teased the sorcerer as he left.

"You, too!"

Robin wished Quadehar would visit him more often. He loved chatting with his sorcerer father just as much as he enjoyed laughing and cuddling with Alicia. But Quadehar had been elected Chief Sorcerer to replace Charfalaq and he had a huge amount of work, rarely leaving Gifdu. Since the section of the *Book of the Stars* considered dangerous had obliterated itself during the famous night on the roof of the temple of Yadigar, relations between the Guild and the Brotherhood of the Wind had improved. And now Quadehar was trying to forge a real bond of friendship and trust between sorcerers and knights. He was also working on a scheme to set up monasteries in The Uncertain World. Apparently, he sometimes went there himself, and people were wondering whether the Guild's first establishment might be opening somewhere near the Purple Forest. . . .

Robin glanced at the alarm clock on the bedside table. Alicia would be arriving soon. She always came around midday. They had lunch together, each with a tray on their knees. Robin had never felt so close to her. He sensed that she was sad not to be his real mother, but at the same time, she was almost ashamed of her joy at being reunited with the man she had never stopped loving, who had left a thief and returned a hero. She wanted to prove to Robin that Kyle would never take his place in her heart. Robin tried to make her understand that none of these past muddles were her fault, and that she had no reason to reproach herself, since she had always loved him. Wasn't he the luckiest of boys? Kushumai had opened her arms to him and allowed him his freedom, he respected and admired Yorwan, Alicia loved him like a son, and at last his father had come back into his life.

He let his thoughts drift for a while. The face of The Shadow came back to him, sinister at first, then terrifying, and then morphing into the features of the Chief Sorcerer, sneering, weary, then petrified as the magic that was keeping him alive had evaporated. The face of another old man flashed into his mind next, that of Eusebio of Gri who had kidnapped him by impersonating Bertram. Quadehar had told him that the Chief Sorcerer of Gri had escaped and vanished, undoubtedly having fled to The Uncertain World. But he had promptly reassured Robin, saying that he wouldn't be able to hide from Kushumai's men for long. The Bear Society had launched a major operation to hunt down Commander Thunku and his adviser, a dangerous priest by the name of Lomgo, who had both disappeared during the siege of Yenibohor.

Kushumai . . . Robin could still picture Amber's expression when she had told him about their conversation, during one of her visits. The Huntress had explained at length the unhoped-for chance that Amber, as a Hamingja — a person who has been bewitched and conditioned — had unwittingly provided to protect Robin. Kushumai had apologized profusely, but Amber realized that the Huntress had done what she felt to be right at the time, and, given the opportunity, she would do it all over again, without considering how painful it was for Amber, or the risks to her physical and mental well-being. This capacity to sacrifice without scruples what she considered small things for the greater good had only reinforced Amber's admiration for this decidedly unusual woman, who was beyond good and evil, like Nature, whose daughter she claimed to be. But she had also aroused in Amber a lasting defiance, and knowing that Kushumai was Robin's real mother made her feel uneasy. "Lucky you've got Quadehar for a father," Amber had teased Robin, "to balance out the genes."

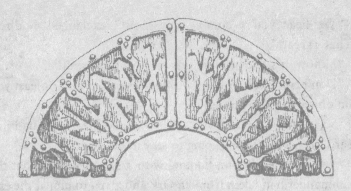

EPILOGUE

"So how's our dear Robin?" asked a nurse cheerfully, entering the room with her arms full of flowers from The Uncertain World.

Robin smiled. She was his favorite nurse. Always smiling, always ready for a laugh, sometimes teasing him until he blushed to the roots of his hair. And, with her shining eyes and dark hair, she reminded him of Amber.

"I think you have visitors," the nurse said, putting the flowers in a big vase.

"Who is it?"

"I don't know," she taunted. "There are two girls and two boys jumping up and down with impatience outside!"

"Oh, that's not funny," said Robin, feigning annoyance. "Tell them to come in."

The nurse left, laughing.

A few moments later, Romaric, Godfrey, Amber, and Coral burst into the room.

"We hear you're coming out soon!" exclaimed Godfrey. "That's great!"

"I know, it's like being in prison. . . . I can't wait!"

"Don't complain, you lucky thing!" said Coral. "At least you don't have to go to school!"

"So it's been decided, has it?" asked Godfrey, who had just heard the news. "Kyle's going to stay in his desert?"

"Yes," replied Robin, fiddling with a sun medallion that the Commander had taken from an Ork and given to him at the end of the battle. "I'll miss him, but I promised to go and see him as often as I can."

"And have you heard about Toti?" said Coral.

"Toti? No, what?"

"He's going to come and live on The Lost Isle," Romaric revealed. "Uncle Urian has decided to adopt him. He finds Penmarch Castle very empty now that Valentino's gone. And as Toti's brother, the archer, died during the battle of Yenibohor, he has no family left in The Uncertain World."

"That's a good idea," said Robin, thrilled. "But tell me, cousin, Uncle Urian's changed a bit, hasn't he?"

"Com-plete-ly! You should have seen him at the big party given by the Provost in honor of the knights! He hugged Yorwan, called him his brother, and asked him to forgive him for having believed him capable of running away when in fact he had performed an act of great courage in sacrificing his happiness to save that of others. It was very moving. He also hugged Mr. Krakal and Mr. Balangru, who have made up their quarrel after their children put them to shame by fighting The Shadow together while they were squabbling over nothing."

"What about Thomas? And Agatha? How are they?"

"Yes, do tell us about Agatha, Godfrey," insisted Romaric, smirking.

"She's fine," replied Godfrey, ignoring the innuendo.

"So is Thomas," said Romaric. "His shoulder and leg are almost healed, and the Brotherhood wrote to him inviting him to enroll at Bromotul next year. That means there'll be at least one decent squire."

"I heard a rumor that you and Agatha are working on a show for the summer, in which she sings love songs and you play the mandolin. Is it true?" asked Romaric.

"The zither," Godfrey corrected him, unruffled.

"Stop it, the two of you," said Robin, laughing. "Is there any news of Bertram?"

His friends exchanged amused looks and Coral burst out laughing.

"You'll never guess . . . ," began Romaric. "You know that Bertram went and asked the Korrigans for help, when we were all trying to rustle up support for the army of the Hills?"

"Yes, my mas . . . my father told me. He even said that the help of the old Korrigan magicians had been crucial in defeating the priests."

"Bertram has always been very evasive as to why the king of the Korrigans agreed to help us fight The Shadow. Do you want to know the best part?"

"Of course. Don't keep us in suspense!"

"In exchange for his help, Bertram promised Kor Mehtar to serve as his personal jester for as many days as the Korrigan magicians were away from Boulegant!"

"You mean . . . that Bertram spent a whole week with the Korrigans, having to act the fool and suffer the king's whims? No! How awful!"

"That explains why he kept wanting us to hurry up in Yenibohor!" it suddenly dawned on Coral.

"Since that episode, which apparently didn't go too badly from what I've heard, Bertram's been in The Uncertain World with Gerald," finished Romaric. "He's helping him with some very important work for the Guild. . . ."

"My . . . my father told me," said Robin, "that when my magic energy and that of the book of spells rose up into space, two new constellations were born and that disrupted the pattern of stars in the sky. For the Graphems to be able to continue working in The Uncertain World, they have to be given a form that matches the new configuration of the stars. It's a huge job. It'll take at least two of them to do it."

"Is it true that you named those two constellations?" asked Coral in awe.

"Yes. I called them the constellation of the Sorcerer and the constellation of the Knight, in memory of Qadwan and Valentino."

"That's really lovely!" approved Coral.

"Hey, Robin," Amber suddenly exclaimed. "I hope you haven't forgotten. . . . You've absolutely got to be out of here by next week. The Provost is planning a huge party for you. There'll be tons of people. The whole of The Lost Isle is invited, and lots of guests from The Uncertain World — the People of the Sea, of the Desert, of the West and of the Purple Forest."

"Don't worry, I wouldn't miss it for anything!"

"Oh," broke in Godfrey, looking at his watch. "We've got to go. If we overstay visiting time, they won't let us back to see you!"

"Fine then, abandon me! And thanks for coming!" Robin exclaimed with a laugh.

Godfrey went out, nudging Amber in front of him. Behind them, Romaric and Coral discreetly held hands, unaware that Robin was watching them with an amused smile.

"Wait!" exclaimed Amber, clapping her hand to her forehead as soon as they were in the corridor. "I forgot something. Go ahead, I'll catch up," she called after her friends.

She marched purposefully into Robin's room and strode over to the bed, much to his amazement.

"I forgot my jacket," she said.

"But you're wearing it!"

"I know."

She leaned over and brought her lips close to Robin's. He was taken aback, but didn't attempt to resist. As their mouths touched, he closed his eyes.

"I'm so glad you're OK."

"Yes, so am I."

"See you tomorrow."

"See you tomorrow."

With a pounding heart, he watched Amber leave.

After his friends had gone, Robin felt empty. He tried to cheer himself up by looking at the many presents he'd been given that he'd placed around his bed, as he used to do with his winter solstice presents when he was younger.

He was fascinated by a beautiful white stone given to him

personally by Kor Mehtar when he had come to visit him as part of an official delegation accompanied by the Provost. The stone was covered with the signs that the Korrigans called Oghams, which were the instruments of a magic that came not from the stars, but from the earth and the moon. He stretched out his hand and stroked it. The stone was polished and smooth. He playfully rubbed one of the Oghams carved on the edge.

Then his let his head sink back onto the pillows, absently biting his lip. He could still taste Amber. Even if the *Book of the Stars* had taken back the magic powers it had bestowed on him, it had given him the most wonderful gift of all by allowing him to live.

On the floor, unbeknown to Robin, the Ogham he had touched had awoken and was beginning to give out a warm red glow. . . .

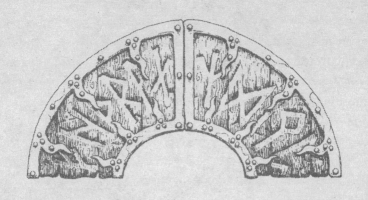

ROBIN'S NOTEBOOK

THE MULTIVERSE

Master Quadehar told me that there are other Worlds beyond the ones we know. Apparently there are nine altogether! He explained that these Worlds are connected by a sort of pillar (not a real one, of course!), the Irmin or Yggdrasill, which is the axis of the Worlds and unites the space in which they move and provides the vital balance that ensures everything works. Finally the Wyrd, the web, links all things to each other, whichever World they belong to. That's why the Sorcerers of the Guild prefer to speak of the multiverse rather than the universe: Even if it is cohesive and sustained by powerful bonds, the universe isn't single, but multiple.

THE INSIGIL

This is a spell that is similar to a Galdr and resembles a Lokk, but is neither one nor the other. The sorcerer invoking an Insigil makes a circle, or wheel, with Graphems. He doesn't link them together and he doesn't mix them, either: He combines them. By combining them in a specific way, the sorcerer causes them to be obliterated in favor of something else. Something independent. Powerful. And dangerous, too! That's why the Insigil is very rarely used. The most famous is the Dragon Insigil, also known as the Lindorm. The Graphems called up during the ritual fade and are replaced by a monster serpent which remains a prisoner in our dimension until it has accomplished its specific mission. And as it can't stand the light, it's in a hurry to obey so it can return to the comforting shadows of the Void as soon as possible. Sadly, Master Qadwan fell victim to the Insigil in The Shadow's tower.

THE ODHR

This is a state of ecstasy, of extreme inspiration, which allows great detachment from reality. The Odhr is the opposite (and the complement) of the Hugr, which represents the conscious mind, total awareness, being fully attuned to reality. It's thanks to the Odhr that I was able to escape from the horrible Tortoise World, and that I didn't need to eat or drink afterward.

THE WORDS OF THE CRIER
FOLLOWED BY THE APPRENTICE
SORCERER'S POEM OF WISDOM

I know that I will remain hanging from the tree
   Windblown
   For nine nights
   Wounded by a sword,
   Delivered unto myself
   Hanging from this tree
   Nobody knows how far its roots reach.

Nobody offered me a drinking horn,
   Nobody gave me any bread.
   I reached out
   I picked up the Graphems,
   Howling I gathered them
   Then fell . . .

Then I began to put down roots
   And learn,
   To grow and prosper.
   From word to word
   Words led me,
   From act to act
   Acts led me.

You will discover the Graphems
    And you will interpret the book
    The book, so important,
    The book, so powerful,
    Written by the Powers,
    Inscribed by the Sage,
    Colored by the Crier.

Know how to write and to interpret,
Feel the colors and the shapes,
When to cast and when to cast off,
Then know your Graphem's measured fate.
Sometimes it's better not to ask the question
When the answer's in the Stars.
Feel the strength as it grows within you
And find your gift will reap its own reward.

THE GRAPHEM ALPHABET

ANSUZ (A)

Position: Fourth Graphem
Other names: the Repulsive, the Humid
Associations: creative powers; intelligence ("sharp as a sword"); knowledge
Powers: unlocks inner powers; reveals the Ond (the breath of life) and leads to the Odhr (inspiration, ecstasy); frees from the fear of death; Graphem of songs and incantations

HAGAL (H)

Position: Ninth Graphem
Other names: the Great Mother, the Star, the Red, Hail
Associations: connects the past and the future ("Hropt created the ancient world"); contains the mysteries of the multiverse
Powers: perhaps the most powerful of all the Graphems; it has many powers; more than any other Graphem it defines the Vey, the sacred space associated with magic practice

SOWELO (s)

Position: Sixteenth Graphem
Other names: the Wheel, the Root
Associations: power ("I bow down to the sacred"); the spirit; contains the power of the sun; shamanic fire; terrifying
Powers: strengthens the will; architect of devastating victories; powerful energy that smashes barriers, frees humanity, and puts it back on the path of its destiny (Orlog)

TEIWAZ (t)

Position: Seventeenth Graphem
Other names: Balance, Light, the Invincible
Associations: external balance (the masculine equivalent of Berkana); justice, harmony ("the smith often uses his bellows"); Graphem of the Irmin, the pillar of the Worlds' Powers; maintains cohesion between things; law and order; balances the forces among themselves

EHWO (ê)

Position: Nineteenth Graphem
Other names: the Horse, the Twins, the Highly Renowned
Associations: harmony between horse and rider ("it is a comfort to those who never rest"); union of the body and the spirit; protector of spiritual quests and vows of loyalty
Powers: assistance in the event of difficulties when traveling between the Worlds; makes it possible to project the spirit outside the body and for the spirit to move within the body; increases speed

MANNAZ (m)

Position: Twentieth Graphem
Other names: the Cosmic Egg, the Ancestor, Mani
Associations: dreams and unconsciousness ("the hundred doctors"); unity of time ("powerful is the falcon's talon"); link between Humans and the Powers
Powers: expands the memory and human potential; protects from chaos

ODALA (o)

Position: Twenty-fourth Graphem
Other names: the Heritage, the Thief
Associations: belonging and possession; center of a clan; secret of a temple
Powers: protects the home ("in its home, the Eagle prospers"); governs inaccessible places; makes it possible to express our innermost feelings ("become what you are")

Constellations that have given birth to Graphems:

THE HERDSMAN (ODALA)

THE HERDSMAN (ODALA)

THE CUP (HAGAL)

CASSIOPEIA (SOWELO)

CASSIOPEIA (SOWELO)